# Choice, Set Free
## Book 5

# The Tae'anaryn & the Spear of the Troll Prince

National Library of Australia Cataloguing-in-Publication entry

| | |
|---|---|
| Author: | Ireland, Joe, author. |
| Title: | The tae'anaryn and the spear of the troll prince |
| Series: | Choice, set free. Book 5 |
| Imprint: | Dr Joe |
| ISBN: | edition one 9780648494102 |
| | This edition, 2nd, 9780645899962 |
| Date: | 3rd July 2024 (1st ed 16th March 2019) |
| Pages: | 252 |
| Size: | 140mm x 216 mm (5.5 x 8.5 in) |
| Spine Width: | 0.528 inches = 13.411 mm |
| Weight: | 0.663 lb = 315 gm |
| Target Audience: | Primary school age. "Middle fiction". |
| Subjects: | Individuality--Juvenile fiction. |
| BISAC: | YAF000000  Young adult fiction |
| Dewey Number: | A823.4         F IRE |
| Lexile Number: | 750 |



                         By Dr Joe Ireland

## About the author

Hi, I'm Dr Joe: philosopher, educator, storyteller.

I am a science education specialist, based in Brisbane, Australia, which means I go about trying to get children (and teachers) to understand how to create knowledge through science. I have a lifelong passion for philosophy (particularly epistemology) science (as a social phenomenon) and fantasy, having written award winning fantasy for the Living Greyhawk campaign setting. I enjoy spending time with my wife and family, attending church, and in challenging people in what they think and in what they think about what they think. I also play flute.

The Tae'anaryn is a thinking book – designed to challenge readers young and old to consider the world they live in. Fantasy novels are a great way to teach, allowing us to explore worlds beyond our reach, to meet people beyond imagining and to take a piece of that experience with us when we return to everyday life. That is what I hope this book will do for you. I hope it will take you on a journey to meet ideas and individuals you might never have the opportunity to meet in any other way. Learn more, discuss, disagree, converse. I hope you enjoy *The Tae'anaryn*.

Sincerely,

Dr Joe Ireland

**More wonderful titles by Creating Science & Dr Joe:**
**Choice, set free.**
*Delightful high fantasy for the thoughtful young reader*

1: The Quest of the Tae'anaryn
2: The Tae'anaryn and the Wizard's Apprentice
3: The Tae'anaryn and the Paladin's Squire
4: The Tae'anaryn and the Enchantress's Chrysalis
5: The Tae'anaryn and the Spear of the Troll Prince
6: The Tae'anaryn and the Khozmoh Djinn
7: The Tae'anaryn and the Voyage of Imagination's Dawn
8: The Tae'anaryn and the Crown of the High King

*Engaging science fiction adventure with real science!*

**Space Chase 1: Arrendrallendriania**
Space Chase 2: Elizabeth
Space Chase 3: Daniel
Space Chase 4: The Mechanizer
Space Chase 5: Moiya
Space Chase 6: Pancake

**Dragon Riders of Pearl**
*Because Dragons…*
Dragon Riders of Pearl 2: Seven Worlds
Dragon Riders of Pearl 3: Return of the Plague
Dragon Riders of Pearl 4: Rage of the Dragonmen
Dragon Riders of Pearl 5: Twilight of the Giants
*Trilling young adult science fantasy adventure.*

*The world's best D&D campaigns – The Wolf in the Sky, Balor's Blade, Quill Versus the Lost Academy of Angelfall, and Hidden city of the Exiles*

*And don't forget – Creating Science, hands on science experiments and activities for everyone! And Dangerous Science, science to blow your minds.*

                    By Dr Joe Ireland

*Dedicated to:*

Every gifted 7-year-old who loves to read chapter books,
especially Vanessa Johnson and Ivy Muldoon!

20, 91, 6, 3, 6  50, 2  1  100, 6, 26, 2, 99, 61

# Contents





By Dr Joe Ireland

# Table of images

## Characters

**Kialessa** – protagonist the story, we see the world through her eyes. She is a tae'anaryn, a race with a demon as one parent. She has red skin that does not burn, small horns, and a tail. But does that mean she's evil, or is that a choice she must make?

**Eclipse** – born of a saintly moon dragon and murderous rot dragon, Eclipse was raised to be the mount of a criminal archmage, Piex's uncle Tobiuus. Now the archmage is defeated and Eclipse does not know where she belongs in the world. Kialessa is the only individual she will fly with.

**Posk** – Kialessa's very good friend, a mentally disabled half-troll boy with exceptional physical strength and speed. He recently acquired a wizard's headband from Piex and can now speak and express himself clearly.

**Piex** – Kialessa's first and best friend, the nation's most talented wizard's apprentice under sagemaster De'Feur. He has made himself a new headband.

**Darrix** – another of Kialessa's best friends, a prayerful warrior. He is now the squire to a famous paladin Tomin, and Darrix is one of the few people in nation who can train and ride a horse.

**Allastassia** – a talented enchantress, and a good friend to 'Kia'. Allastassia successfully recently underwent her chrysalis to become an even more powerful enchantress, and is well on her way to become one of the most powerful enchanters in the world.

          By Dr Joe Ireland

## The kingdom of Lenmer'el

**King Dunnkan** – the kind king of the nation. His closest advisers and personal bodyguard consist of:

**The Steward, Lord Grudon Fletcherson** – the king's steward, in charge of running the day-to-day affairs of the kingdom. He is a human / part fey of unknown origin.

**High Captain Bon Sure'e** – the human captain of the king's army, strongest and most skilled warrior in Lenmer'el.

**Sagemaster Lord Cour De'Feur** – high wizard of Lenmer'el, an elf. National expert on things arcane, including the sciences of magic and alchemy.

**High Priestess Lady Jacinthia Stonehall** – a dwarf, priestess of the Eternal, highest religious authority in the kingdom.

## Troll characters

**Ki-Taieri** – an ambitious troll king who seeks the throne of all trolls in order to restart the war of 300 years ago.

**High shamaness Jindalessa** – wife to Ki-Taieri by right of battle. She watches over her people with great concern.

**General** – An unnamed troll military genius whose support of Ki-Taieri will be vital to his goal.

**Liturgist** – a musician priest, whose role it is to remember sacred texts and music for their people.

**Beast master** – a coveted role among the trolls, only the wisest and best may become a beast master. They raise and train beasts for battle.

**Troll sages** – rare, yet equal the wisdom and knowledge of any human sage, troll sages, "Never accrue the fame their work deserves," according to sagemaster Cour De'Feur.

**TotoMuru** – (TotoRore to some troll scholars) the ancient troll warlord and hero. Three hundred years ago he rose up with his fellow slaves to overthrow their human overlords, and almost succeed in destroying the entire human kingdom.

# Glossary

Babbling – muttering constantly

Bastard – a child whose parents aren't married to each other. In medieval times, a terrible social crime, and often an excuse to be mean and unfair to the child.

Doleful – sorry, regretful

Abject – complete, total

Ambiance - the local mood or background

Conjecture – an educated guess

Condescend - to do something you think you are otherwise too important to do

Communicated – literally, 'to move'. We usually use it nowadays to mean 'move information'

Deigned – condescend

Dialogue – a two-way conversation

Din – a lot of noise

Distended – stretched out from the inside, bloated

Efficacy – ability to produce intended result

Incessant – without interruption

Indulgence – with lots of luxuries and not very many rules

Inestimable – too large to be calculated

Irrepressible – unable to be restrained

Magnanimous – very, very generous and forgiving

Neutralise – render inert or ineffective

Obeisance – worship and obedience

Singular notion – one, compelling, thought

Sloven - lazy

Smidgen – a tiny bit (an informal word)

Temerity – fearfully

Temporarily – limited, not permanent

Tremulous – shaking or quivering, also relates to being nervous

Unadulterated – without anything added, pure, 'unchanged'

   By Dr Joe Ireland

# Belonging

*Until you risk presenting your sincere, vulnerable, and imperfect self to the judgment of an indifferent world, you will never find a place to belong.*

*Bon Sure'e, captain of the king's guard, 313CY*

The horizon burned red with the fires of war. The entire bank of the river, as far as could be seen in either direction, was scorched and black. Terrifying symbols, words and curses in troll speech, were scratched into the corpse of every burnt-out tree. It was clear; the troll hoards were coming...

Kialessa stood with the others, looking out in silent fear as the Broadwaters River turned the colour of blood.

And from that crimson surface the black stained forms of the troll elite had emerged.

'Draw your swords!' Noe-esk commanded, unable to keep the trembling from his voice.

'Why here, why now?' Allastassia screamed, lightning forming around her hands.

Kialessa and her closest friends had been sent out, with a dozen other trained warriors of the king's guard. Sent to the safest, least likely, location along the coast of the Broadwaters to warn if any trolls attempted to cross; a terrifying reality none of them expected, but which they now all had to face.

'Come trolls, and face death at my hands!' Mayalee, the guard commander, shouted.

'Target their necks!' Noe-esk reminded them. 'Remember; they heal quickly, and are strong. Do not let any live that fall, and do not let any land a direct blow!'

The instant the trolls left the river, they broke into a run. In that moment Kialessa realised just how futile this all was. The trolls where massing in their thousands, while there was barely thirty of them.

With blood curdling roars the fastest among them raced to the battle, eager for human blood. They were there in moments. The first few of them raging head on towards them.

Suddenly momentary confusion reigned as a *vivid starclash* hit their forward forces head on, stalling the first eager trolls in their forward charge. An instant later

 By Dr Joe Ireland

blinding wave of lightning tore through their ranks, dozens falling to the most powerful enactment of Allastassia's enchantments Kialessa had ever seen. None in reach were spared the unrepentant blades of Lenmer'el. As fast as the trolls where, it was clear they did not expect the sudden skill and determination of the handful of soldiers and students of Lenmer'el. The wall of shields held against the bloodied axes, and trained soldiers parried the field of spears that struck against them.

The defenders formed a tight circle, and Kialessa knew they would soon be crushed together as the hoard thickened around them.

Darrix must have guessed it too, a moment later there was a stunning screech, and the paladin's squire rode out on his enormous beast right over the defender's heads. He charged forwards and into the hoard. He drove them back with the blinding white fire of his shield, his sword parrying spears with miraculous power.

'No!' the Mayalee shouted, 'this is not the time for heroics, boy!'

Yet in the next moment Posk took the cue, his eyes black pools of rage, and leapt out on his drake, sundering axe and spear with his enchanted gauntlets. With a cheer the defenders noticed the hoard pull back several paces. The mounted defenders prowled around the wall of shields, daring any to approach their island of silver steel in a sea of black bloodlust.

And it was such a very small island. Kialessa tried to

get a shot out with her bow, but it was impossible in the writhing mess of limbs to get a clear shot. She felt so helpless.

The trolls were a horrifying army. Green skin and tusks painted black, their weapons dyed red. They roared savagely, threatening them with tusks of bone.

Then there was the baleful call of a troll horn, and in the next moment, the hoard stood back, grinning cruelly.

All fell silent.

The commander took a moment to whisper, 'I have just received word that the hoard has met our main forces at the high hill. The battle is joined.'

'What do these wait for?' another soldier muttered, a cut above his brow.

The hoard began to part, and a moment later a single, muscular troll was seen walking towards them. Unlike the others, he was not crouched down, and his form was very man-like in appearance. He was strong and broad, with the noble bearing of a prince. At his side he dragged a single weapon; a large, curved black sword doused in flickering green flames.

'Who is that?' Allastassia asked.

'The warlord *himself*,' their commander stated, and for the first time, real fear clung to her voice.

Kialessa briefly wondered how they'd gotten into this situation.

'Well,' stated Eclipse in a voice that almost sounded bored. 'This seems like as good a time as any…'

                    By Dr Joe Ireland

*Your chance to change the world will come, my dear.*
*Elven Queensage – Sagesse L'aimé, 316CY.*

Kialessa ran down the line of caravans, dodging the soldiers who with dower, grave expressions were loading them for war. Tail flicking, she ran her excited hand along the spokes of the wheels as she nimbly leapt out of everyone's way, usually before they even noticed she was passing by.

It wasn't the news of war that made her run, or the

urgency to be anywhere in particular. Danger; real danger, loomed. The college had been cancelled for the rest of the year. Kialessa listened as soldiers boasted of how many trolls they would personally slay; their talk a mix of respect and disdain for the legendary troll strength. They knew what to expect, but to Kialessa it all seemed too unreal. War, and any real danger, seemed so far away from the bold soldiers and polished swords within the castle of Lenmer'el.

She was so distracted that she almost bailed face first into one of her best friends, Posk, the half troll.

'Oh, hey, Tauira,' he called her one of his favourite terms for her, meaning "tutor". She smiled back at him. It was good to hear him talk, not last season and he'd been too mentally injured to speak at all. Now he wore a wizard's headband, and could speak, and no longer crouched down but stood up on his feet like the other young men.

But Kialessa was surprised to see Posk's expression. He looked flustered. 'What are you up to, Posk?'

His hands wrung with concern even as he stepped close to her to avoid two soldiers rolling along an enormous wheel. They shouted at him to get out of the way.

'Big guys got the wood. Metal lady doesn't need the steel moved. Um… guess I was just looking for a way to help.'

Kialessa looked around at the mayhem of soldiers

                      By Dr Joe Ireland

preparing for war. She didn't even know what *she* was supposed to do.

But Posk was half troll, and a boy at that. This was not a safe place for him to be, all good intentions notwithstanding.

Posk continued. 'I cut some wood, they loaded it there.' He pointed. 'Got it done too quick. Tried to help load the meat, but I think they thought I was just trying to steal it.'

He showed her his hand. Someone had struck a rod against it. She knew from experience it'd be fine in a few days, by the next dawn if he healed like most trolls did.

She patted it in sympathy. 'You don't belong here Posk. You need to wait out in the forest until the war is over.'

Posk sniffed. 'Yeah. Wait. Belong? What makes you think I don't belong here?'

She felt nervous about that. 'It's with trolls, Posk. The trolls are coming to war.'

Posk looked around. 'Then these squishy men are definitely going to need me,' he concluded. 'You think I don't belong here?'

'No, you do, Posk. Maybe just not right here, right now. You should…' she wanted to say, "wait out in the forest," like she had tried to the last time an army came to town, but she just didn't feel right about it. If Posk wanted to help, he surely could. 'Maybe you can see what Darrix needs?'

Posk nodded. 'You will see. I am not afraid. I know these tall men with their staring eyes do not like me. I can tell they are all a little afraid today, and is it because I remind them of their enemies? Hmm. Yet it is here that I live. My forest is their forest. If I do not belong here, then where?'

Kialessa didn't know what to say.

'And what does it mean to belong?' Posk wondered out loud. 'And what does one do, once one finds where they belong?'

She smiled at him. He always had such amazing questions now that he could speak.

'I'm going to the horses to see if Darrix needs me to move the old straw again.' Posk decided, not even checking to see if his "tutor" agreed. 'There's a big fight coming. I'm coming to that too!'

Another heavy wagon lumbered by and they stepped out of the way. 'Yeah, good call.'

'Children!' a voice shouted out from behind her. Kialessa spun around, and was relieved to see it was her friend, the soldier Noe-esk. He was brushing down Riumi, his battle posk, while others unloaded the cart of newly forged weapons the animal had been pulling to the war caravans.

Kialessa ducked under a long catapult arm that was being carried by five men, running to greet him. 'Gentle!' She smiled, grabbing his open hand. He was one of the few humans who didn't cringe at her touch.

     By Dr Joe Ireland

He smiled down at her. 'Whatever are a pair of students from the king's college doing playing among the soldiers?' he asked, head to one side in gentle accusation.

Posk shuffled around to cover her back-to-back, just like in combat training, as if he expected the battle to start any moment.

'I …' she didn't know what to say.

'You just wanted to see what was happening,' he guessed.

She looked down at his feet, 'Well … actually, I did hope someone would have something that we could do. College is cancelled, and I can just imagine all the girls in the dormitory right now,' she sighed. 'They'll be sitting on their beds discussing who will do what, and who they hope won't die. I just can't be like that. We need to do something, not sit around talking about those who do!'

He smiled, and messed her hair, ignoring the looks other soldiers might have given him for touching a tae'anaryn. She liked him, her officer Noe-esk.

Posk looked over his shoulder, and nodded with a grunt.

'I suppose,' he began, 'you could help me brush down Riumi here. She's been at work all day. Not a complaint, mind you! Tougher than stone, my beast,' and then she heard him mutter under his breath, 'I would risk my life to save her.'

Kialessa patted the massive posk, who leaned affectionately against her. She flung her arms around

Riumi's enormous neck, grabbing the brush Noe-esk offered, and began brushing the thick matted fur in silence. How easily posk's thick fur could become matted in the wilderness! Most ended up with shortened fur, not so effective against weapons, but much safer against the cutting burs of spiked seeds and overhanging branches. Posk followed her moves with a brush of his own, a look of deep concentration on his face.

A soldier's voice sounded out from among the din, course and authoritative, 'Step it up, warriors!' the woman shouted. 'Captain of the king's guard wants this done by midnight, and at this rate you'll all be here till dawn!'

Kialessa knelt down, hoping the commander didn't see them. There wasn't any particular animosity between her and commander Mayalee. But the woman who'd been charged with taking Kialessa from her parent's inn and to the college at the start of the year never seemed pleased to see her.

'Move on, move on!' the commander continued to shout. 'Everyone must do their part!'

Kialessa hid, brushing Riumi silently as she listened to the sounds of preparation around her. Just yesterday she had been studying and practicing with everyone else her age at the college. Then the horns had sounded. Within the hour messengers had come running down from the keep to all parts of the land. From that hour class had been cancelled, and no one had told her where to go, or what to do. Kialessa had never seen war, but she knew it was coming. Everyone knew something was coming, if not by the assassination attempt on the King's life that she had personally foiled, then by the failed attempt by demons to enforce religious tyranny in their land. In a strange sense … it was calming to have something to focus her energy on.

1 Kialessa pats Riumi the posk

She whispered to Noe-esk while he fed Riumi, 'What do you suppose is going to happen?'

He sighed, moving closer so they could hear him clearly, and to perhaps give them some cover, 'You heard the news. The trolls are massing for war. We're heading to the Broadwaters river that divide our lands from the trolls. There king Dunnkan hopes kind words, and a show of force, may yet offer us a diplomatic solution. Hopefully … we can stop this war before it even begins.'

'Do you think it will work?' she asked.

'We can only pray,' he replied.

'Bah!' the commander scoffed suddenly from behind her, making Kialessa jump. How she had managed to sneak up on them was a mystery.

She spoke to Noe-esk, 'Don't give the children false hopes, boy.'

Kialessa was bothered at her tone.

'Why? Don't you think we will win?' Posk teased.

Kialessa nodded, 'There are five troll nations, and seventeen of us in the Great Kingdom.'

The woman glared at them. 'Oh, we'll win,' she replied. 'But due to the peace treaty of the past three hundred years, which I have always known was a great mistake, their numbers are now vast. Each troll nation is twice the size of any individual kingdom of the Great Kingdom. If that were all we would easily win, but trolls both young and old come to war: each is able to draw twice the number of soldiers than the average kingdom. They outnumber us *twenty to seventeen.*'

'Please, sir,' Noe-esk said softly, and she huffed. He turned to Kialessa, 'Mind not her fears, youth.'

'Fear? I do not fear,' commander Mayalee replied. 'I

     By Dr Joe Ireland

just thought you'd like to know what were up against. We will prevail, but the cost will be great. And if the trolls have some new magic, some new show of power, or new allies … let's just say we may be all the worse than last time.'

'Last time?' Posk asked.

'Yes, *last time* the trolls invaded, child,' she emphasised with a clenched fist. 'Three hundred years ago under TotoMuru; Blood Lord. Oh sure, we won. And it may have resulted in the birth of the Great Kingdom under Emerel. But it also resulted in the death of one in every five people. Think on *that,* little half breed.'

'I think I'd rather not.'

Noe-esk set to adjusting Riumi's harness.

Commander Mayalee continued, seeming to enjoy the attention, 'Who knows what surprise they have that makes them bold this time? A new weapon? A new tactic, a-'

'Dragon!!' Noe-esk shouted, drawing his spear.

His shout sent shockwaves of pandemonium and fear along the ranks. There were twenty heavy war caravans, all together in the central field of the keep, all being laden with equipment and provisions for war. There were over a hundred soldiers, too busy preparing to be properly armed, or armoured. That was when Kialessa realised how vulnerable they were out in the open.

It was the perfect time for a surprise attack.

A sudden screech split the air from the far wall of the castle, a shattering discord of primal violence. Kialessa almost heard words in that unholy noise, but also realised from experience that whatever dragon made it would have to be young, and fairly small.

The sound startled Riumi, and despite her training she roared and stood up on her hind legs, slashing the air with razor sharp claws.

And that was when Kialessa saw the dragon, silhouetted against the sky. It was small, as dragons go, with broad wings and wide antlers.

2 At the horizon

That was when Kialessa realised she knew this dragon.

Guards where shouting, running in a panic all around, trying to form a barrier of spears and shields against it from behind the protection of the wagons. They probably hoped it might take one of the animals as payment, but few dragons risked attacking a human castle without expecting much more than that.

 By Dr Joe Ireland

The dragon turned in the sky, and with a screech headed right towards her. Within instants, before the soldiers had even had chance to load their bows, it had landed. Kialessa looked at the large wings, and immediately recognised the dark, narrow snout. The mischievous twinkle in her eyes. The dark, eclipsed moon between her antlers.

But Noe-esk didn't, 'Back! Back you **beast**!' he shouted without a trace of fear in his voice. He lunged forward with the spear, showing he was prepared to use it.

The dragon looked at him with a mix of confusion and disdain, 'Stand aside, human man,' she ordered him with a voice that sounded almost… bored.

'Never!' he demanded. 'Get back to the sky, tell your troll lords to withdraw their designs or face death at our hands!'

The dragon actually laughed. Kialessa looked about. There were soldiers everywhere, cowering behind the imagined safety of the wagons. They had bows drawn tight in trembling fingers, spears held out in sweaty hands. But none of them, none, had the courage to stand against the dragon alone, as Noe-esk now did.

The dragon laughed again, 'You actually think I serve the troll lords? You're more stupid than I imagined. Get me the tae'anaryn. I have business alone with Kialessa.'

Posk grabbed her hand, but she shook it away.

'Noe-esk!' Kialessa shouted, trying desperately to get his attention. But it must have been drowned out by

Riumi's thunderous growls; she could not get free of the wagon, but the posk still turned to face a dragon with her rider's courage.

'NO!' Noe-esk roared. 'You'll never take this little one from her guardians again!' And with that, he threw his spear at Eclipse, the half-moon dragon, and Kialessa's friend.

She barely moved, but allowed the spear to strike her. To everyone's surprise, it actually struck true, making a great gash under what might have been her third rib. By the strength of her scales, and the blessing of the Eternal, it did not strike deep enough to seriously wound her, and Eclipse brushed it aside.

'Ouch!' Eclipse protested, 'that actually *hurt*.'

She took a step back, crouching into a battle position.

Noe-esk hadn't wasted a moment, having already drawn his sword, and had begun already to charge.

'Stop!' Kialessa shouted in desperation, her shrill voice echoing against the castle walls.

Everyone turned.

Kialessa ran to stand between them, embracing Eclipse. 'Enough,' she ordered them both. Then she spoke to Eclipse, 'You've made your point.'

Noe-esk looked confused.

'She is my friend,' Kialessa explained to him.

He still looked doubtful, but indicated the others should lower their weapons too.

Few did.

     By Dr Joe Ireland

'Perhaps,' Kialessa whispered in Eclipse's ear, 'you ought to show them.'

The dragon huffed, rubbing her side as though it hurt. Then Kialessa felt a gentle shifting in the air, and recognised a healer's prayer. Eclipse's wound sealed in a moment, though it still looked deep red.

'You've learned your mother's faith,' Kialessa wondered.

'Some of it,' Eclipse replied. She looked out at the armed and frightened soldiers. She still held her ribs.

Then she stood up tall, taking a slow breath. As she let it out her features began to change. Her neck grew short, her claws into hands. Hair sprung up where scales had been, and by what magic Kialessa was unaware, a simple dark grey dress wove itself from the air around her. She looked different, more mature. Her eyes were now an iridescent blue, her skin porcelain blue, and she wore a necklace of inestimable wealth. She looked taller than before, and, like always, she looked like royalty.

'You ...' Noe-esk breathed in shock, kneeling in a warrior's apology. 'Eclipse, daughter of the moon dragon. I am so, *so*, sorry. I had no idea.'

She walked up to him, her nose in the air, and let the warrior wait on her silence. 'Whatever,' she eventually said in a cold voice, and ignored him.

Posk looked very relieved, he'd met Eclipse earlier that year but they'd never spoken. He stood back, acting cautious, the brush still in his hand.

3 Kialessa the Tae'anaryn, and Eclipse, the part Moon, part Rot dragon

Eclipse turned, and then threw her arms Kialessa, eyeing the warriors carefully as they lowered their weapons in confusion. 'You don't need to be afraid,' she told them all. 'I bring a message from my mother a sky dragon for your king. He would be wise to hear it soon.'

'Yes, he would!' Kialessa beamed. She was glad people were beginning to calm down. War was brewing, people

    By Dr Joe Ireland

were already tense, and her friend who was a dragon decides to show up in person and start shouting?

It was a wonder they didn't charge her all at once.

Kialessa turned to the assembled warriors, still standing around and looking like they weren't sure what to do. 'We need to see the king, now!' she shouted.

Immediately commander Mayalee leaped up, gathering six high ranking soldiers to her side. They offered to provide an honour escort, Posk tagging along.

Eclipse nodded, seeming pleased to have an honour guard. Yet as she walked on she glanced down at Noe-esk and growled at him. But the sound that came out was nothing like it should have been for a girl that looked about twelve. It shook the ground, as though the earth herself was warning all of them to be more wary of whom they thought it wise to attack.

***

By the time they reached the inner keep the messengers had already arrived. Ever since yesterday the bronze statues that stood by the king's throne room had drawn their swords, and now their unliving metals eyes turned to glared openly at any who passed.

Inside, the throne room was a buzz of organised chaos. People talked quickly, in hurried voices. Pages ran to and fro. Beasts of the air, summoned or called, arrived at the windows to speed messages far and wide. And while

Kialessa watched a dryad's spirit conferred briefly with the steward, and nodding, teleported away in a shower of petals and dandelions.

But the room inside fell silent as they entered.

Kialessa noted the king's four closest advisors stood, literally, quite close to him right now. She knew their powerful defences could spring to life in an instant to protect her king.

The steward took it upon himself to introduce them to the silent crowd. 'Honoured King Dunnkan, keeper of the people of Lenmer'el. I give you Eclipse, daughter of the moon dragon Norius, and her friends, Kialessa, the tae'anaryn. And, um, Posk the, ah… half troll.' Even he sounded like he wasn't sure where Posk belonged either.

The king gave a mild, but polite, bow. He spoke to Eclipse. 'We are honoured, young one. It has been quite a while since a dragon stood in this hall.'

Eclipse looked around with disdain, as if to say, *Yeah and I can see why.* But instead, when she spoke, it was with politeness, underwritten with a subtle power that betrayed her inhuman heritage. 'The honour is mine, good king,' she replied with a gentle curtsey, and people in the room seemed to breathe a sigh of relief. 'I bring word from my mother,' the young dragon stated, though with a sigh as if this all bored her personally, 'which I expect you will find comforting. She bids you know the dragons of the sky are mindful of your situation. She confirms that the troll hoards are massing for the destruction of Lenmer'el and

   By Dr Joe Ireland

the Great Kingdom.' And here people still gasped, 'Mother admires your courage for seeking a peaceful solution to this situation, and sends her personal assistance. And that assistance… is me.'

The royalty in the room muttered, and Kialessa couldn't tell if it was good or bad.

'Forgive me, young dragon,' the captain blurted out, 'but aren't you half rot dragon as well?'

The priestess gave him a withering stare, and the king seemed embarrassed.

Eclipse waited a moment before replying. 'Has Kialessa been so briefly among you, that you still judge by race alone? Or are you humans really still too *stupid*? I am descended from the Vaulted Heights on my mother's orders to assist you. If that is not enough help, then in Lumos' name, send me back! I have better things to do than wallow among small minded and short-lived folk.'

Those assembled stirred at her insulting words.

The guard captain nodded, not apologising at all, as if she'd just passed some test.

'Listen,' Eclipse whispered, 'do you want my mother's help, or not?'

The king nodded, 'We are grateful for any help we can find at this time, and more especially from the sky dragons.'

Eclipse nodded, 'Yes, you will be. You are alone, and cannot hope to stem the tide massing at your doorstep. They will overrun your land as fast as they can walk. If war comes to Emerel through this means, Lenmer'el will no longer stand as a nation.'

'Of this truth,' the priestess muttered, 'we are all very well aware.'

'Well, what would the sky dragons have us do?' the king asked.

Eclipse sighed, 'My mother is possessed of the singular notion that I must attend this war. In person. And she insists, despite all your prejudices, that Kialessa come with me.'

The room stirred once more.

The steward took it upon himself to answer. 'It is not uncommon for the young warriors, the squires or an honoured dame, to attend a battle. They are always kept at the edge of the field. They are not permitted in the conflict.'

King Dunnkan interrupted, 'I hope, I *trust*, your mother expects no more than that of our children?'

Eclipse turned to face Kialessa. She had no idea what she was thinking, and certainly why she was making this such an uncomfortable experience for everyone. Eclipse answered, looking back at the steward. 'I fully expect so. Frankly, I see little wisdom in her words or prophecy. I expect our contribution to be minimal. Perhaps we are simply sent as good luck? We … my mother and I have not seen eye to eye of late. It was clear to me that she was glad to see me go.'

King Dunnkan held his peace.

          By Dr Joe Ireland

Again, the captain spoke up, 'The field of battle is no place to mind children, even those with might as unmatched as the dragon.'

It should have been insulting, but Eclipse just huffed. 'And yet… here we stand.'

'It could be convenient,' the wizard proposed, 'conveying messages, areal oversight and the like.'

If Eclipse considered these tasks beneath her dignity, it did not show. Perhaps she was indeed here to help out, however she could. Just like Posk.

The king paused. 'Very well,' he finally said, 'Eclipse, daughter of the moon dragon Norius and murderer Txlax. You are welcomed into the combined forces of Lenmer'el and Emerel. You are to report to Grudon, steward and commander of the information division of this war.'

'It is well,' she replied, sounding a little bored again.

But King Dunnkan was not finished. He took a step down towards her, eyes widened, voice trembling with sincerity, 'And for your mother's sake, for all our sakes: stay out of harm's way little ones! To die in war I can live with, but to see the look in your mother's eyes if you were to come to any grief, I think my heart would break! Stay out of harm's way, young ones! Consider this your most important instruction: *Do not get hurt!*'

Eclipse scoffed, which seemed unimaginably disrespectful to Kialessa.

The steward had had enough of her manners and began to usher them out of the room.

But Kialessa was worried. How could the young dragon take a king's concerned command so lightly? Had she already forgotten what one driven man with a spear had done to her side?

 By Dr Joe Ireland

# The Army Departs

*Never seek war, for war soon enough will seek you.*
*However… carry a sharp spear at all times.*
*Troll sage, Chatuk, unknown date.*

The caravan rode out the next morning: two hundred soldiers, more than half of Lenmer'el's army. Their pennants held high, their shields bright in the morning sun. Kialessa was excited to be riding along with the other youth in the supply caravan right behind the king's carriage. Some of the older students from the college were there too, but they insisted on riding with the soldiers rather than the "little ones".

King Dunnkan himself rode at the head of the army, chin held high, expression resolute, rod of Lenmer'el in his hands. His face so fearless it would set terror into the heart of any troll or demon in their path.

People of all races and kinds lined the streets to see them depart. The aged, the infirm, or those too young to go to war. Many merchants and the commoners as well. Kialessa could see them all holding weapons, their cheers to their king inspiring. But she knew they would all have their own thoughts; of who would live, and who they might never see again. A young family wept, their mother holding out a scarf to the young, metal clad soldier who rode by them. He must have only been about eighteen. He took the token with grace, his own eyes moist with tears, but his jaw set resolute.

The carriage she was on lurched and Kialessa turned to see Posk jumping up from the ground to sit beside her. It usually meant he wanted to chat, or that he wanted some advice. He smelt very much like he'd been sleeping outside all night in a tree again. But he'd grown a lot in the past year. His green hair was now so long Kialessa had to plat it almost daily.

'So! We're going to the big fight now then?'

She wasn't sure what he meant. 'It's called a war, and it's not quite soon. It will take us more than two weeks to arrive there, and there is no paved road where we are going.'

     

Posk looked puzzled. 'But it's a big fight, yes?'

She sighed. 'We hope not. There are too many trolls, we'd never win.'

He scoffed. 'Many, more, most. It doesn't matter. We can still win. I can still win. Just gotta be faster. Stronger. You'll see, Tauira.' He called her by his favourite title for her.

She smiled at him. She was glad he seemed to have cheered up, and liked his enthusiasm. But it was easy to be enthusiastic journeys away from danger and surrounded by friends and family. She hoped he would never lose that courage. 'Good. You go get them, Posk.'

He smiled. 'So why she come along?' he asked in his faltering Emerellian, pointing at Eclipse who rode lazily in the sky above them. The young dragon ignored the four bronze eagles and the elven elite that rode them, part of the diplomatic envoy from elven lands sworn to protect their nation in such situations. Kialessa wasn't too sure how good Eclipse's hearing was, but she was pretty sure she could hear Posk talking, if she bothered listening.

'She's here on a message from the sky dragons.'

'You mean… there's more!' he said, still looking upwards. 'I never seen a … dragon… oh yes, in classes yes, on the pictures. Drakes with wings.'

'I sure hope we don't see any more dragons,' Kialessa admitted, but that reminded her, 'Will Huffy be coming along?' Huffy was the name Posk had recently given to the wild drake he'd tamed, much to the chagrin of the town guard who had never had to let a drake into college grounds before. But Huffy loved the baked chicken bones. Posk had no trouble calling him whenever they felt like another wrestle. They were like pigs in mud, all claws and fists. Kialessa could never tell what was for real, and what was for fun. Drakes, it seemed, were fearlessly loyal once they found a companion.

Posk looked confused. 'Of course, he's out there,' he pointed like it was the most obvious thing in the world. To Kialessa's eyes there was only forest. 'I saw him an hour ago, he's following. Nice Huffy! He's such a good boy! Shall I call him?'

Kialessa looked at the nervous posks, and remembered how badly they reacted to the site of a flying dragon recently, 'Maybe not till we clear the city, and then not till we are quite a few paces away from the army, if that's all right.'

He looked around and thought for a moment, 'Good idea, Tauira.' He kept looking around, his movements fast and enthusiastic. 'She's brushing her hair again,' he announced with a grin.

Kialessa looked over, and noticed Allastassia was indeed brushing down her hair. Just two days ago it had announced the arrival of autumn by turning a brilliant ginger, one of the side effects of being a part dryad enchantress. 'I'm probably not supposed to tell you this, but that's how she practices her enchantress's powers.'

He just stared at Allastassia, who ignored him just like

     By Dr Joe Ireland

always.

'I wish she'd let me use her hair as my pillow at night. I bet it would be the softest, *smoothest* pillow in the world.'

Kialessa wasn't sure how to answer that. Posk had a huge crush on Allastassia, and probably always would. Even so, it was a pretty mature comment for a ten-year-old, but trolls aged much faster than humans so he was probably more like fourteen. Sometimes.

Posk turned to look at the army, banner held high. He caught sight of Darrix riding Mask near the front, and tried to wave to him too, but the paladin's squire stalwartly ignored him. 'What's his problem,' Posk scowled.

Kialessa laughed, 'Darrix is riding patrol, Posk, he's supposed to be focused.'

'Looks boring.'

'It's a parade, a celebration Posk. Some of these soldiers-'

Before she could finish her sentence Posk stated, 'This is how you celebrate!' Stood up in the carriage seat, put his arms in the air, and roared.

The crowd couldn't decide if they should laugh or cheer, but Posk enjoyed it.

She dragged him back down, and couldn't help but smile. It seemed to her that Posk never stopped himself from having as much fun as he could, even if it broke a few traditions.

4 Posk demonstrates how to celebrate

He sat down with such enthusiasm the entire carriage rocked, and one of the posks mooed in protest. Allastassia scowled, but Kialessa laughed.

Next Posk shoved his face up to Piex's nose, which was buried deep in the book he was reading. 'What 'ch read'n?' he asked.

Piex answered by reading out loud, '*Datum munus et inde est, et inde munus illius antiderivati refert ad originale munus.*'

'That makes no sense to me!' Posk celebrated.

Without looking up, Piex replied, reading at the same

 By Dr Joe Ireland

time as speaking, 'I'm attempting to learn the advanced arithmetic necessary for casting the *mage's fiery conflagration*. It requires the calculation of the convergence of infinite sequences to a pre-defined limit, except it must be made in real time, depending on local environmental conditions and astrological considerations.'

'That also made no sense to me!' Posk shouted with a grin, and slapped him on the back.

Piex looked like he almost stopped breathing, but recovered quickly, 'I'm learning to blow things up using fire.'

Posk's eyes grew wide, 'Woah! You... seriously? Serendipitous!'

Piex looked at him suspiciously.

'Sorry,' Posk replied, 'Your old headband I'm wearing sometimes come up with the strangest words for things. I meant... I guess it's lucky you're learning to explode things with fire, it might really help out in the big fight.'

Piex looked chagrined, 'Two weeks is not long enough to master the fiery conflagration.'

'Can you turn me invisible yet?' she teased him.

Piex huffed, 'No! Marchan explained it all to me and I still can't get it! None of it makes sense, it's a bizarre contradiction of believing in the unbelievable and wizardry doesn't work like that! I just think he got lucky.'

'You'll get it,' she said, secretly glad Marchan was somewhere in the other carriages. But she knew what he was talking about, wizardry being very complex and all.

Piex had even read out to her the entire scroll he'd given her, and explained every glyph and symbol, but she still couldn't cast her own *magesight* spell. She could barely add two numbers together, and there were some weird relationships involving the lengths and angles of triangles.

Then Posk jumped up and started singing,

*'Two hundred men of sword and steel!*
*Off to the troll lands, trolls to kiiill!*
*Slice them! Dice them! Cut them true!*
*Or else, you know, they're gonna cut yoouuu!'*

'That rhyme is pathetic!' Allastassia squealed, looking up just to chasten him.

He was silent for a moment, 'Got *your* attention!'

'Oh, you! Why are you even dressed like that! Put on a shirt, Posk!'

'Nice hair you got there, flamey!'

'You…' she was momentarily lost for words.

They kept it up for the next hour, arguing with each other, criticising each other's battle tactics and personal appearances. It eventually got the point where even Piex's legendary concentration was tested.

'She really does enjoy arguing with him,' Piex observed.

'He really does love the attention,' Kialessa agreed.

Piex sighed. 'He has a point about her ignoring her rear flank once her ice shield enchantment is activated.'

It made Kialessa wonder, Posk was one of the few who

　　　　By Dr Joe Ireland

seemed to be able to get things through to Allastassia. Perhaps it was because he was willing to do anything to get it, or perhaps it was because he didn't care how badly she thought of him. He was just Posk, no matter what anyone said.

Eclipse floated down. Kialessa was beginning to think she didn't use her wings to fly very much, more to steer. She seemed to swim through the air like most other sky dragons. 'While I might otherwise agree to a discussion of battle tactics, must we endure this doleful dialogue further?' she criticised them.

Posk grinned, and Allastassia simmered.

'Can you travel thought the night?' Posk blurted out.

'I can travel whenever I want,' she replied, sounding irritated.

'No, I mean, um, like… oh, this stupid headband doesn't have words for this.'

'Good, perhaps then we may not long have to endure your incessant babbling!' she chastised them, and flew back up.

Allastassia glared angrily at her.

Even Posk seemed troubled, a little. 'She's got a baaaad attitude,' he said to Allastassia, more than loud enough for Eclipse to hear. 'Why is she even here?

'One wonders *where* she belongs,' Allastassia mattered in offhand cruelty.

*If you wish to win a war, you mustn't be afraid to lose a battle or two.*
*Humdug, dwarf scholar.*

It was obvious that none but Kialessa was going to ride with Eclipse; the dragon made that abundantly clear by threatening to eat anyone who suggested otherwise.

Almost two weeks had passed. Kialessa and Eclipse rode now, high in the sky, with only an elven warrior on a giant eagle for company, barely within earshot.

For a long time they simply flew in silence, watching

the horizon for signs of enemy trolls. Kialessa's legs were just starting to become a little stiff; Eclipse having adamantly refused to be saddled or harnessed in any way, when the mixed blood dragon spoke, 'Are you enjoying the view?'

'Yes,' Kialessa admitted, though she was wondering what Eclipse meant. Perhaps she was just trying to make conversation.

'It seems ironic, doesn't it?' Eclipse continued. 'I am breed to be the mount of a powerful wizard, and yet as I grow, I bear a tae'anaryn.'

Kialessa smiled, hoping she meant well. 'Yes, both of us have strange histories.'

'Well, yes, that as well I suppose,' Eclipse said. 'It does me good, however, to be out here in the air.'

'Me too!' Kialessa agreed. When she didn't look down, it was fun to feel the wind always blowing against her face, exhilarating to feel but not to see the sudden shifts of height as Eclipse communicated through the air. Flying was a great delight.

'And,' Eclipse continued as though thinking to herself, 'I suppose it feels good to be helping.'

Kialessa was a little struck by that, 'What is this?' she said with false mockery, 'Eclipse, the mighty dragon, enjoying herself being helpful?'

The dragon laughed, and glanced at her, 'What, does this surprise you? I still have my mother's heart. You humans are so beneath me, you are *lucky* I'm here to help out.'

Kialessa waited a moment before replying, 'It's not that, isn't it, Eclipse? You can blame your heritage all you want but you still get to make your own choices. You are choosing to be helpful simply because you can. Sometimes it's nice to be helpful, just to know that you can make a difference.'

'Pah,' Eclipse disagreed, seeming to try and become grumpy again, 'my mother is forcing me to do this.'

'Is she, really?' Kialessa argued. 'If I've learned anything about you, it's that you would never let your mother make you do anything. Go on, admit it, you *like* helping.'

Kialessa knew she had her. It was impossible to feel grumpy when flying, and this was one thing they both knew Eclipse had a rare and special talent for, and she was sharing that talent right now with a group of humans that really needed it. And she wasn't being paid to be here, it was purely voluntary. And somehow, deep inside, even Eclipse couldn't deny that made her feel good about herself... maybe just a little.

The dragon laughed softly, seeming to admit defeat, 'Cunning little Tae'anaryn,' she protested.

Suddenly the eagle veered dangerously upward in the sky. The elf warrior drew his spear and began to set it in his saddle even as he called a warning to them both.

Eclipse banked in the sky, and they both looked around frantically.

 By Dr Joe Ireland

'There!' Eclipse shouted, pointing with her snout and preparing to go into a steep dive.

Beneath them, tearing directly up at them with impossible speed, was a black griffon. It had no rider, but still bore a terrible cunning and malevolence in its eyes. Dark feathers fell from the air behind it as it rocketed towards them at an unbelievable speed.

5 Eclipse v's the griffin

Swifter than she thought was possible Kialessa swung her steel bow around and prepared to nock an arrow. But the far end of the bow caught on Eclipse's wing, and by the time she had righted it, it was already too late. It would have been better to have simply thrown something.

With a horrifying screech the griffon tore into them, and in spite herself Kialessa shut her eyes, expecting to the thrown from her dragon's back and begin a life-threatening plummet towards the earth below. But somehow Eclipse seemed to evade the collision, though with a terrifying jolt she felt the bow torn out of her hands. By the time Kialessa had blinked the griffin was high above them, hurtling towards the elf and his eagle.

'After them!' Kialessa screamed, and with a thunderous battle cry, Eclipse raced after them.

The griffin had slowed down to normal now, but was still in rapid pursuit. The elf launched two arrows with great skill, and one struck the griffin's feathered chest but fell immediately away. The beast was closing in on the elf quickly.

'Faster!' Kialessa cried.

They shot after the monster, but it was still closing too fast on the elf. The eagle was dodging with amazing skill, but the griffin was strong. Then, just as it snatched forwards in an attempt to impale the man, he did something amazing. The elf leapt up from his saddle even as the eagle spun downwards. Slashing with his sword, he did a backflip in the air, and barely missed the griffin's flailing head. The monster roared and flapped frantically to regain its height.

Eclipse almost ploughed head on into it. 'Now!' she

     

told Kialessa.

There wasn't even any time to say, "Sorry, I dropped the bow," before Eclipse and the griffin were exchanging frantic claw slashes in the air. Kialessa couldn't even tell what had happened, but by the time they'd recovered a deep black slash ran across Eclipse's tail.

'Sharper than I thought,' the dragon admitted.

'I dropped the bow,' Kialessa confessed.

'You… what? What good are you now!' Eclipse screamed at her.

Kialessa didn't have an answer, but drew her whip instead. She cracked it in warning, not sure how to use it in a battle like this one.

The griffin had recovered from their collision, and by the look of the excess number of feathers fluttering to the ground Eclipse hadn't done too badly herself.

The griffin turned towards the elf once more. It seemed to shrink into itself, curled its wings in and yet magically did not fall. Then its eyes began to glow a vibrant, dire green.

'Sorcery!' Eclipse gasped.

Kialessa had heard of it happening. That just as some people like Allastassia were born closer to magic than others, so too were some beasts. With the right training and care it could be a good thing. With an evil influence it would lead them right to sorcery.

Again the griffin shot up into the sky, trailing feathers in its wake. The eagle and the elf hardly had a moment to ready themselves. He set his spear, but the monster collided with him head on. There was a shriek as the spear went right into the griffon's shoulder, but the elf was torn violently from the saddle and began to plummet silently towards the ground. The eagle took after him immediately.

'Now, while the sorcery has drained him!' Eclipse shouted, and charged. There was no hint of fear or temerity. She wanted to claim her victory, and no riderless griffin was going to get in her way.

Eclipse surged after the griffin, roaring a battle cry. It was in the act of chasing after the eagle, but dodged away when it saw a dragon chasing it. Within instants it was down among the trees, dodging them with incredible skill.

Eclipse chased it frantically, breathing heavily. She screamed another battle cry, her voice becoming more bestial and monstrous. But the griffin was gradually evading them. She tried to anticipate its movement, but it slipped into the shadows.

For a moment Eclipse hesitated. Her breathing frantic, her pupil's dilated, her claws fully extended.

Kialessa was momentarily more terrified by the sudden and bestial change in her friend than she was of a hidden griffin.

'Let it go,' Kialessa half pleaded, 'we need to-'

'No,' Eclipse hissed. 'I will not be bested by a mere griffin!' Her voice barely sounded like her own, as if some demon had possessed her, and she would rather die than let her enemy escape.

It made Kialessa very nervous.

Eclipse shot upwards, clearing the upper branches of the forest in a heartbeat. She surveyed the landscape intently.

Kialessa didn't know what to say, but kept the whip curled and ready.

Eclipse grew more silent, her wingbeats slowed. It was as if she was holding her breath.

And just as she fully expected, the griffin rocketed out of the underbrush an instant later with its magically enhanced speed. An instant before it could collide with them Eclipse projectile vomited her flesh-eating dragon acid all over it.

The griffin screamed in horror. Kialessa could only imagine the agony it must have felt drenched in a bucket load of rot dragon spittle all over it. Tiny droplets fell against Kialessa's hand and arm, stinging her painfully. She rubbed them franticly away, and then she realised she was falling.

She screamed, and an instant later Eclipse had grabbed her ankle. Together they scurried to right her up on her dragon's back again, Kialessa not wasting a thought on what could have happened. Eclipse looked like she wanted to say something like, *Stupid tae'anaryn, I told you to stay on!* But it looked like the griffin had knocked all the wind out of her, and it was all she could do just to stay upright.

Weakly, Eclipse followed the griffin. It was in full retreat now; its wings tattered from the dragon's breath, its underside and shoulder pierced by many wounds.

Kialessa didn't bother wasting her time trying to convince Eclipse to let it go. They followed it for a good half hour, seeming unable to catch up with it as it fled. Kialessa wondered where it was going, till she suddenly noticed a bright sliver of sunlight reflecting off a large river.

'It's heading for the Broadwater,' Kialessa realised.

Eclipse stopped her forward flight. Together they looked toward the horizon. The sky was darkened with the smoke of fire. Hundreds upon hundreds of trolls would be camping just beyond the river. Even from this distance, Kialessa fancied she could hear the clash of their weapons preparing for war.

'They're camped right up against the river!' Eclipse said with an element of surprise in her voice.

'Do you think they see us?' Kialessa said, allowing the concern in her voice. They were in no condition to fight once more.

'No, we'd know already,' Eclipse replied, seeming to float even lower in the sky.

'Let it go. We've seen all we need to.'

For a moment Eclipse paused, seeming intent to push on. Then she cursed, 'Useless elf. If he wasn't so pathetic we'd have caught that monster by now.'

Kialessa was silent. She'd been really impressed with

    By Dr Joe Ireland

the elf and his brave eagle. And now she and Eclipse were far, very far, from their assigned route. They were closer to the trolls than they should be. And Eclipse looked so weary that she'd lose a battle with a sick rabbit.

Words could not express her relief when Eclipse turned around, and flew back to the safety of the waiting army.

# Diplomacy

*Owning your story can be hard, but not nearly as difficult as spending your life running from it.*
*Jindalessa, high shamaness and queen.*

'They're what!' the steward roared.

'I cannot believe you did not hear what we said,' Eclipse said, chin held high. 'So I have to assume you are too thick to understand it: The entire troll army is camped right up against the Broadwaters river. And we can confirm the ranger's report – I clearly saw banners from all *five* troll nations.'

The steward didn't waste time being offended, but

   By Dr Joe Ireland

groaned audibly and slapped his hand to his forehead. Turning to the king, he said, 'Your highness. This is most inadvisable. They out number us ten thousand to one. You should not even *be* here!'

King Dunnkan stood, and spoke abruptly, 'If there stands even a hint of a chance for peace, for my people and theirs, I will seek it! Send a messenger. We are going to call for a negotiation as soon as we arrive.'

'But… that will be tomorrow evening…' the steward muttered.

'Indeed, it will.'

***

Kialessa sat among the coals in the fire, turning the roasting pig on a spit. She did not like to get the ashes on her armour, though it would clean itself within a few hours, so she sat on a stone and reached in to turn the burning embers by hand. It did not feel like much of a contribution to an army, but it was something she could do. And by now the humans were used to the sight of her cooking for them.

The camp was silent now, waiting for the night. Double shifts of armed and armoured warriors patrolled the area, set on a high hill and fortified with hastily constructed barricades. Kialessa put more faith in the high stone the priestess had raised and blessed, and the banner of the king that stood before them all. But in her heart

Kialessa did not think there could come any danger to them tonight.

Posk sat, watching the soldiers remove a carriage wheel to reset the steel rim. Darrix was shining some armour, rubbing the metal with slow, meditative purpose. Shining armour was the only down-time the paladin's squire ever got. Allastassia was helping some of the others to sort and mend blankets and tents, magic tingling from her fingers as torn thread sewed itself together at her whim. And Piex sat close by, holding a mage book in his hand, but staring up at the stars without speaking.

'What are you doing?' Kialessa asked him – she needed some conversation.

'Math,' he replied.

'Math?' she wondered, forgetting for a moment that he didn't need stylus and slate for the task.

He nodded. 'Differential calculus in real time is not very easy. Master bids me practice.' He turned a small, ten instants hourglass on the top of his book. 'It is a difficult algorithm, and the danger to the caster is very real. Multiple variables must be considered, and too little or too much of any may result in the energies igniting within the caster. There! 24.27,' he checked his book and the small hourglass still running there, 'Excellent!'

It almost belayed the fact that none his age, ever, had been known to achieve that feat.

'You should teach me numbers, as well,' she told him.

'You understand numbers sufficiently well for the

          By Dr Joe Ireland

tasks that are required you,' he replied.

It was the kind of dismissive answer she was used to. 'Don't you think it might simply be good, to simply know?'

That was when Eclipse spoke, her voice dry and accusing. 'Knowledge without purpose is a bitter well.'

Kialessa looked over at the young woman. She had been meditating, or something similar. She had not said anything for hours, not since the battle with the black griffon had gone so poorly. Since then Kialessa had learnt that the griffon did have a rider at one point, but the elf had, indeed, seen to it. But since that report Eclipse had said nothing, and simply sat, allowing the world to move on around her.

'A bitter well?' Piex asked.

'A sage spoke it, a dragon, long ago. Who was it, Nemethis or someone, I don't remember.'

'I know the quote,' Piex replied, seeming actually a little put out. 'I believed it applies to trivial knowledge, gossip and the like. Not to the mathematics required to conflagrate a small army.'

'And you expect Kialessa to be able to do that someday, do you?' Eclipse said, a condemning accusation staring out from the one eye she deigned to open at him.

He chose not to answer.

She huffed, and went on meditating.

A person approached; it was one of the page boys from the castle. Kialessa tried to remember his name before she realised she'd never heard it, but it was the young man who'd come and got her the day the captain had given her the acid dagger. It still rested in the chest back at the castle, but Kialessa was confident she could retrieve it in a thought through the Shadowrealm. Perhaps she should ask Allastassia who this young man was; he was probably a lesser noble to have an important castle job already.

'The steward wishes to see you,' he muttered, not looking at her, but staring instead into the hot coals she was quite comfortably resting her feet among.

'Very well,' she replied.

He took up a large wooden shield and held it out against the flames. He reached out his hand to help her up, but she was already standing by the time. 'Oh,' he said, standing to let her pass.

'The breeze is light tonight, but cool. So keep that fire high, all right?'

He didn't look at her as she spoke, but instead tried to drag a cooler stone close to sit on. She wasn't sure what he was thinking, probably something like why she was trying to tell him how to do his job and turn a spit. He probably knew how to do that quite well.

Chagrined at her folly, she walked quickly away. To her surprise she found the steward only a few tents back, and not at the command pavilion. He was accompanied by four of the king's guard, and openly held the rod of Lenmer'el, which was good. Kialessa knew she was one of the only people in the kingdom who could touch that rod

     By Dr Joe Ireland

without coming to harm.

She was almost tempted to take it out of his hands and wave it around a few times just to see if some new power appeared. Maybe something useful against trolls.

He stepped forward and with a friendly grin stooped down to whisper to her. 'Dame Kialessa, an honour it is to see you tonight. We are glad you did not come to any harm, though it was certainly a very dangerous situation.'

'Nothing any good soul would not have done,' she said, giving a diplomatic curtsey Allastassia had taught her.

To her surprise, he actually scowled. 'Oh child, you're beginning to sound like that Greens'holm girl! No, no, no. I come to you for a bit of honesty, it's what our king so often says he values about you.'

'… All right,' she replied, wondering what he wanted.

He sighed, 'You weren't in any dire danger, were you?'

That was very confusing, 'There's a troll hoard massing less than a day away. We're all in very real danger, aren't we?'

He laughed quietly to the night, 'Yes, yes, we are. All right, you're nothing if not irrepressible, aren't you, Kialessa. And, you are right, nothing more than any right-thinking person would have done as well. Very well, I see my charge to keep you safe was never really in my power to do so, anyway.' He paused, 'Thank you, by the way, for the information you brought us today.'

She nodded, 'But it was Eclipse that must be thanked,

she risked more.'

He nodded, seeming again a little serious. 'Yes, that does bring me to my other concern. That dragon friend of yours, congratulations, by the way; dragons make friends for life. Anyway, how is our little dragon, Child of the Sky?'

Kialessa thought carefully before answering. 'She is child also of the Rot; she is quick to remind all that she is a half caste, like most tae'anaryl. And all that is necessary to understanding who she is.'

'A unique being, that is sure,' the steward agreed with a diplomatic nod. 'But my question still remains; how do you think she is doing?'

She felt burdened by the question, and did not want to answer. 'She will always be a being of cruelty… and of patience…'

He waited.

She sighed, 'But I fear she is a little… distracted at the moment. I think her relationship with her mother is troubling her, in some way. She is … it's like she's *looking* for a fight.'

The steward nodded, 'We noticed. The captain was the first to notice it, and the priestess confirms it. Have you seen her hands of late? The skin around her eyes?'

She did not know what he meant.

'Stretched, tired. Thin. Kialessa, we think she's beginning her great sleep. It's the time a dragon sheds their skin, then goes to sleep for a few years, and when



By Dr Joe Ireland

they wake up, they're a new size. It would explain her moodiness, and the tension with her mother.'

Kialessa nodded, it would make sense. She looked up at him, wanting to know more.

He knew what she meant, 'We should expect some more bad behaviour from her, for a while, until she simply succumbs to a dragon's need to sleep. Mood changes, strange behaviours. Sudden cravings for weird and unpalatable foods. As a child of both a Sky dragon, and a Fell dragon, we are not sure what to expect. But your companion Piex has studied all the books on dragons in Lenmer'el, he should be able to give us some pointers that might be of assistance. Will you ask him for us? I'm authorised to provide any assistance the young dragon requires.'

'Why don't you just ask her yourself?' asked Kialessa, it seemed the most obvious thing to do.

'I get the impression that I'm not her most favourite person in the world right now. I didn't want to seem interfering. But to be honest, I'm not sure she even knows of her condition at the moment, or has admitted it to herself.'

*Not again*, thought Kialessa. *Another friend about to break the world, or change.* But then again, she'd not done too badly helping someone though a life change by simply being there. Maybe that was simply what life was like.

The steward looked down at her, becoming serious once again. 'She has left her mother's nest, and sought you out among all the beings in this world, Kialessa. I don't know how helpful that will be towards our cause right now, but I can hope for the best. Please, just let us know what we can do to help our little dragon, it's the least we can do when her mother trusts us with her.'

'I will,' Kialessa promised herself, and them.

'Thank you, young woman. I admit; I had my reservations about you when we first met. But now, I think you're beginning to grow on me, young dame.'

And with that, a man who once dreaded to touch her now placed his hand on her shoulder, and shook it with comradery, as he might a soldier's.

Her face lit up with a grin at the compliment she didn't know she'd needed, and with a mutual nod, she skipped away into the night.

***

Kialessa though him the bravest man in the whole entire world. King Dunnkan stood, with not one but all four of his closest advisors, on a hastily constructed barge in the middle of the Broadwaters river. On the near side of the river, two hundred soldiers of the Great Kingdom stood in double file. They seemed to Kialessa to be standing on their toes, they looked so tall. Their shields were polished, their helmets gleaming. They looked an intimidating force.

On the other side of the Broadwaters crouched several

         By Dr Joe Ireland

thousand trolls. They were covered in mud, their leather armour died in blood. They roared in chaotic confusion, spitting and swearing, tearing up great clumps of dirt and throwing them in the river. They were the troll elite. Each bulged with muscles, and a few of them were huge, up to three times the height of a normal human.

King Dunnkan said nothing, but motioned for the steward to stand forward.

'King Dunnkan, honoured keeper of the people of Lenmer'el, seeks to speak with the noble leader of the troll hoards! We invite you to parlay.'

The trolls roared, as though insulted.

'They're not coming,' the captain muttered. 'And we will be first to die.'

A moment later their numbers began to part. There, standing at the water's edge, was a single female troll. She had the noble bearing of a queen, with a bone and feather head dress to match. She had a vulture skull staff, and numerous tattoos and markings across her skin.

'A shamaness,' Darrix muttered, his voice full of concern.

Beside her a lanky troll general stood; a head taller than any human Kialessa had seen, but his eyes full of an unusual cunning for one of his race.

At her command the troll general spread out a wide, thick carpet onto the river. To Kialessa's surprise, it floated. And when the troll shamaness stepped on to it, it held as firm as a wooden raft.

To the cries and swearing of the troll army, the troll general took a great staff, and joining her on their raft pushed off from the bank. They floated to within arm's distance of the king's raft. The shamaness held up her arm, and the troll hoard slowly fell silent. Kialessa found she had to strive with all her might to hear what they were saying.

'I am Jindalessa, troll wife to the warlord Ki-Taieri. Welcome to the far end of the Broadwaters, red king of men,' she said with a cunning smile.

For a moment, King Dunnkan was silent. Then he spoke, 'Tell me, lady Jindalessa, why has your king gathered this hoard?'

'Why? For blood and glory, no less,' she said, then spat with disdain, as though she hated her own king. 'He wants to be famous. To write his name all across the history of thinking beings. To shake the world to its foundations and then, I suppose, to become immortal. That is why, and what has changed? He is just as ambitious as any man I have ever met.'

'I do not understand,' King Dunnkan said, looking puzzled.

The troll shamaness sighed, 'These past three hundred years you have lived in peace. We trolls have stayed in our own lands, warring among ourselves as is our right. Yet this generation has been different… then it produces Ki-Taieri. With his strength and charisma he has now concurred the five nations among the trolls. Now he seeks

   By Dr Joe Ireland

to turn them against the East. He wants to rule the entire world. If you'd paid more attention, you might have noticed this long before it got to this point.'

King Dunnkan's brow furrowed, and Kialessa doubted he was unaware, especially with such experienced prophets among his own people.

'But you don't pay attention, do you?' the shamaness continued. 'And now, Ki-Taieri claims the right of the blood lord.

'What?' the captain said with a derisive air.

'Exactly!' the shamaness replied. 'The same reason TotoMuru claimed as an excuse to go to war against you, and we all know how well it worked for him... millions of us will die, mostly my brother trolls.'

'If you are so unimpressed,' the priestess said, 'why do you not stand against him?'

The troll shamaness huffed, seeming not at all offended or put off by the suggestion of rebellion. 'Why? Because it is not my place. It is against our law. That is why. There is nothing he lacks now but the authority to command all the troll hoards, and then they will attack. None of you will live to see winter's end when that happens.'

'Is there no dissuading him?' the steward asked.

The shamaness sighed, 'I have told you all you need to know, and all he commanded me to tell you. Prepare for your deaths.'

With that, she commanded her general to take her

back. King Dunnkan spoke after her, 'Then let us discuss the terms of this battle. If we cannot convince him to abandon his design.'

'Meet me again here tomorrow evening, I will talk,' she told him.

As soon as they were out of ear shot, the steward muttered, 'She is stalling for time. If they come to talk tomorrow, it will be as fruitless as it was today.'

'Spread the soldiers out,' the king commanded. 'Even if at best we hope to stall them but one hour, it will be time we buy our families and kingdom.'

The priestess replied, 'Yes, sire. But the trolls intend to come for war. There will be no stopping this. They will attack tomorrow morning.'

     By Dr Joe Ireland

# The Battle

*Never demand a miracle, but expect them.  A flower will bloom in its own time, and is there any greater wonder in all of nature?*

*Lady Jacinthia, High Priestess of Lenmer'el, 313 CY*

They came the next day.

Kialessa stood with the others, looking out in silent fear as the Broadwaters river turned the colour of blood. And from that crimson surface the black stained forms of the troll elite warriors were emerging.

'Draw your swords!' Noe-esk commanded, unable to keep the trembling from his voice.

'Why here, why now?' Allastassia screamed, lightning sizzling from her fingertips as thorns sprouted at her feet.

The battle was there in moments, and they only barely managed to hold off the troll hoard. Posk and Darrix patrolled their flanks, holding the slavering monsters at bay.

But it was a fragile standoff, and one that could never last.

The hoard began to part, and a moment later a single, muscled troll was seen walking toward them. Unlike the others, he was not crouched down, and his form was very man-like in appearance. He was the size of a normal human, with incredibly broad chest. He had the noble bearing of a prince and a crown of gold and bone on his brow. At his side he dragged a single weapon, a large, curved black sword doused in flickering green flames.

'Who is that?' Allastassia asked.

'The warlord himself,' commander Mayalee stated, and for the first time, real fear clung to her voice.

Kialessa briefly wondered how they'd gotten into this situation.

'Well,' stated Eclipse, 'this seems like as good a time as any.'

Eclipse turned herself into a dragon and leapt up off the ground. Kialessa squealed as she wrapped her claws around her arms and lifted her high into the air with a wing beat so powerful it almost flattened the defenders. She hefted Kialessa on to her back, and their climb

    By Dr Joe Ireland

continued as the trolls watched on with battle wariness.

'What are you doing?' Kialessa clutched on in panic. It looked like they were flying away.

'A favour for my mother.' Her voice was dark and threatening. 'Let the trolls consider their folly.'

An instant later Kialessa saw the first of the griffons the trolls rode tearing through the air toward them. She hoped Eclipse had a plan.

She was not disappointed.

The black dragon spread her wings. 'Now;' she instructed Kialessa, 'scream.'

Kialessa filled her lungs with air, then she screamed for all she was worth, her deafening screech shattering across the sky with surprising power. Suddenly the entire horizon, from one end to the other, was filled with a powerful vision. It was the sign of the white dawn; the sign the trolls had first seen the day their ancient war lord TotoMuru was slain.

The effect was immediate. The griffin riders stalled, the black elite struggled to hold their weapons.

While the massive army on the far side of the Broadwaters stopped dead. Hundreds of trolls on this side of the bank turned and fled back toward their lands.

With slow circles Eclipse floated back down to the centre of the circle of steel-clad warriors of Lenmer'el. No one dared to take their eyes off the confused trolls while they shouted to each other in their strange langue.

But Mayalee spoke, 'What was that, dragon?'

Eclipse turned back into a human, seeming quite relaxed now. 'A gift from my mother. The trolls know now that the dragons of the sky do not support their cause, this time. They will pull back, or those that don't will be easily slain by the king and his soldiers.'

The warriors began to cheer, but Mayalee silenced them, 'Do not add insult to their loss,' she warned them.

But the near trolls weren't retreating, at least, those painted black did not. They turned, and looked around at their rapidly thinning numbers.

And through the hoard Kialessa saw their warlord. He looked at the sky, then down at her.

And he grinned, as though he knew a secret that would get him what he wanted anyway.

Then he turned, and walked away.

Immediately the trolls began to flee. It was only a few moments before they had all fled across the Broadwaters and back into their own lands.

Then they cheered.

***

No-esk was testing the bandage on his arm. It had been scathed by a troll arrow.

The guard captain walked by to check his work.

'It will make it hard to hold my shield arm until it is fully mended,' he confessed.

'You'll have to wait for healing,' Captain Mayalee told

him. 'The priestesses have had too much to do already today. Still, I'm impressed that you fought the poison off on your own.' She checked his binding, and without another word walked away.

They waited by the fires. Sounds were becoming muted by the night as most of the warriors turned in for sleep. Kialessa felt safe, their camp surrounded at all times by two dozen armed soldiers, ready to battle at a breath's notice. And in the centre of their tents the king's pavilion rested, and within, the greatest warriors in the entire kingdom. And one of those, the steward, held the rod of Lenmer'el, which contained the promise of every citizen of the kingdom to care for and protect each other. Kialessa felt almost as safe as she ever had in stone walls at the castle. With the hope of their recent victory it seemed this show of faith might even be enough to stop a war.

That was when Kialessa heard a stirring. While sharp spears turned skyward, Eclipse alighted from the air. The dragon could see as well as Kialessa in the pure darkness, and was probably returning from a self-appointed surveillance of the nearby lands. Kialessa watched as the dress formed around the young woman, as the dark hair sprang up and grew from her scalp. Within only a heartbeat Eclipse the human stood there.

She looked exhausted, and miserable. She must have been aware that Kialessa was watching, but said nothing. Instead she just sat down at the other end of the fire, hidden in the shadows of a tent.

Kialessa wondered why she did not join her. The night was getting cool. They should all turn in for rest soon. Kialessa looked up into the night sky, towards the waxing crescent of the moon, Lumos. It was a very bright night, even for this hour. Kialessa thought how Eclipse's mother must be up there now, and wondered if she was watching.

Then she realised where Eclipse had seated herself; in the shadow of the tent, far from her mother's gaze. She sat in deep silence, arms wrapped around her chest. She did not even stir as the last two soldiers left, leaving only themselves and Noe-esk.

Night-time seemed to deepen around the young lady, and it looked to Kialessa that silver tears rimmed her eyes.

Noe-esk motioned towards the dragon with his head.

Kialessa walked around, still sitting in the moonlight, within an arm's reach of Eclipse. 'Are you all right,' Kialessa asked.

Eclipse just huffed, as if to say, *Of COURSE I am not,* but said nothing, and went back to staring into the fire.

'The moon is very bright tonight,' Noe-esk offered.

Eclipse glared at him.

He went on with whittling a piece of wood, perhaps to keep his injured arm exercised.

Eclipse hugged her knees. For a long moment no one spoke, till she said, 'I shouldn't even be here.'

'Well, I'm glad you're here,' Kialessa told her, trying to cheer her up.

Eclipse huffed again, 'I did my chore. You people don't

          By Dr Joe Ireland

even count… how I hate my mother.'

Kialessa was shocked to hear that, but didn't know what to say.

Eclipse filled the silence. 'I met Lumos, and Serros. They both gave me their blessing. The star king even showed me his entire kingdom. They said they have a place picked out for me… that there's a chair with my name on it.'

'Sounds good, this is good, right?' Kialessa offered.

Eclipse continued, 'But they can't speak for all their people. I saw it, the fear. The hidden glances at the "rot bastard"… besides, their cities are too bright. There are no shadows there.'

Kialessa waited in silence.

'I'm just so mad at her,' Eclipse admitted, kicking the ground. 'She thinks she knows everything about me. They don't know anything about me. I have to "control my temper", I have to "show more compassion", I have to "stop eating the cutlery". It's so annoying.'

Kialessa wanted to say, "Aren't all parents like that?" but held her peace.

'My own mother is ashamed of me. She hid for ten years in a dungeon, too afraid to escape… too afraid to see what I really was.'

Kialessa was upset by that, it was everything **but true**. She wanted to say something, but knew some feelings were just for hearing, not fixing.

'They **don't** like me, and I **don't** belong there,' Eclipse muttered.

'Where will you go?' Kialessa asked.

In reply, Eclipse started crying, soft sobs that barely pierced the night.

Without waiting to be asked, Kialessa lent over, and gave her a gentle hug. Without really meaning to, Kialessa wrapped the shadows of the night around them, till they must have been completely hidden in the darkness. They stayed there till Eclipse fell asleep, curled up like a puppy in the dirt.

Kialessa joined the soldiers of the watch that night, and did not sleep as she watched over her friend till dawn's pale message finally began to light the far horizon.



By Dr Joe Ireland

6 Without a home

# The Training

*A short temper makes a quick fool of any solider.*
*Tomin, Arch Paladin of Serros, 314 CY.*

Eclipse's mood just got worse and worse. By the next evening Kialessa could *feel* the ire surrounding her. Everything she did showed a distinct desire to not be here. The trolls had not returned to attack, which was fortunate. But the mood in camp was tense. Few spoke, and all watched.

Once more Kialessa and her friends sat by the fire, warming themselves.

'You are fortunate they have not manifested any

          By Dr Joe Ireland

alliances with dragons, as yet,' Eclipse stated.

'Why is that?' Allastassia asked.

'Because, part fey enchantress, then your cause would truly fail. Were the Nature dragons or, curse the word, Fell dragons to take sides, the only mercy would be that this war would be over much quicker. The least of my kind is far superior to any of you humans.'

'Oh, is that so?' commander Mayalee mocked, standing up. 'Perhaps you'll put that on a little wager for me, youngling?'

Eclipse just stared at her, the daytime echoing her silence.

Commander Mayalee rested her hand on her sword.

It was impossible to predict Eclipse's first attack. She exploded from the log with such force it flew backwards, knocking everyone to the ground. She was half transformed by the time she reached the commander, and clobbered her on the jaw with an outstretched claw. Bleeding from her mouth the arrogant solider screamed, and was pinned an instant later to the ground by a still shifting dragon. Her antlers folded out, the dark moon arising between them and covering the area with a dark light. Her huge limbs, bigger than Kialessa seemed to remember them, stretched out. Eclipse seemed cold, wreathed in indignation and anger like a frozen lake that had just taken its first kill.

The soldiers grabbed up sharpened swords, swinging their shields in place. Eclipse gave them all the time they needed.

'Dragon, you don't need to do this,' Allastassia begged.

'Time for some humans to learn some humility,' Eclipse answered, and then, without looking, whipped out her tail with such speed and ferocity it not only knocked the swords from two soldier's hands, but knocked them painfully to the ground as well.

The other soldiers reacted with speed and accuracy, born of hours of training. But somehow they must have been a half instant apart, for still Eclipse found ways to dodge and avoid them, her claws and tail scything around sundering blades, slashing armour, and knocked full grown men to the ground. She did, however, refuse to bite anyone.

The battle was brief. In the last Mayalee was holding back, looking for a moment to strike. The instant Eclipse turned her head, she took it. But it was all a ruse; her dragon hearing was exceptional in the extreme. Eclipse dodged down, and lifted her wing up against the soldier's arm. There was an audible crack as the commander Mayalee's arm broke, and her sword flung away and buried itself deep in the ground.

The commander cried out, and knelt down.

Eclipse growled, and towered over her.

'Enough!' a commanding voice shouted. It was the captain of the king's guard. 'What is the meaning of this?'

Eclipse backed down slowly. 'A little lesson,' she told



By Dr Joe Ireland

them.

'Is that so, dragon?' the captain replied. It was clear he was angry. 'One that wastes the healing of the priests? And that wounds my soldiers!'

'Your soldiers are *pathetic!*' Eclipse roared, tendrils of black fire folding from her snout. 'They have nothing to offer the troll hoard in resistance! You are all dead, you hear me! Dead in a breath without my help!'

Eclipse sounded so confident, yet after she'd done speaking she bowed, as if she couldn't believe what she'd just said. But it also looked like she just couldn't help herself, or she truly believed it.

'Is that so?' the captain stated. His voice was soft, and measured. In a word; dangerous.

Eclipse growled. The ground trembled at her pent up, irrational, rage.

From behind the captain, from the shadows, emerged six human soldiers in full battle armour. They had the tall gold and blue plumes of the king's guard, the royal crest on their shield and matching pommels on their swords. They were the king's honour guard; who do not fear dragons. And they carried with them an aura of nobility, confidence, and skill.

The captain nodded, and as one, they grabbed the hilts of their swords.

Everyone panicked, dragging anything valuable or injured as far away as possible. Two tents were even ripped up from their stakes and simply dragged away.

Within an instant the ground was clear.

'You don't need this lesson,' the captain stated, 'but you've insulted the honour of our kingdom this night, and since we might die tomorrow, I cannot allow that to go unchallenged. Yes, you are powerful, young dragon. But do not think yourself invulnerable. And do not, ever, think we human's exist only at your whim, and have no ability to defend ourselves. King's guard, teach this arrogant young dragon of the strength of Lenmer'el.'

Eclipse growled, crouching down, ready to spring into battle again.

'Eclipse –' Kialessa tried to reason with her, but the dark dragon turned and glared at her. Within her eyes, all wisdom was gone, replaced only with the bitter hatred of her rot dragon heritage. Her breath was rank, and the moon above her head almost invisible.

The captain turned his back on them all.

And Eclipse leapt.

It was a poor tactic against the elite. The two at the front swung the flat of their swords against her wrists, jarring them painfully so that she fell to the ground in a tangled heap. By then they already had her surrounded.

But being surrounded was not as much a disadvantage to a dragon as it might have been to another creature. Simultaneously she lashed out at each foe, and simultaneously they shielded or avoided the attack. She swung her tail out in a fierce curve, but one solider simply stepped forward and prevented her from getting enough speed up to hurt anyone. Before she could wrap him up he'd leapt out leaving only his sword. She cried out as she cut herself on it.

As one they stood forward and battered her.

A moment later she lunged forward, concentrating all her power on the man right before her. Twice he dodged her flailing blows, and in frustration she gripped his shield with her teeth. He had released it before she could throw him and, in the moment between realising the tactic had failed and developing a new one, he punched her right across the face.

Eclipse roared, and two soldiers leapt on her back. She stumbled under their combined weight. Writhing and twisting with incredible ferocity she managed to fling them off, and with unexpected speed spread her wings and managed to just take off.

For a moment she seemed to hover in the air, too exhausted to attack, too proud to flee.

So she breathed on them.

The white glittering shards of magic exploded from her mouth, scattering in all directions and dousing the king's guard in an instant. Kialessa only waited a heartbeat before the wind swept that magic her way. Every nerve went numb, every sensation seemed to abandon her limbs. It was the legendary breath of the moon dragons.

And it was not enough to stop the king's guard. Only one seemed unable or unwilling to move. Another bent down, and a moment one of his companion's ran towards him. She put her foot in his hands, and he hefted her high into the air.

Eclipse was unprepared for the tactic. The heavily armoured solider landed solidly on her back, holding her sharpened, magical blade against the raging dragon's neck. In the same movement, she stomped against Eclipse's shoulder blades, right between the wings.

The young dragon cried out in dismay and pain, and crashed to the ground.

The remaining guard had her pinned in moments.

The captain walked up to her. 'I should have you thrown out for insubordination, youngling. You are a dishonour to your mother's name. You are a poor choice for your mother's gift, even though it saved our lives. You have no place teaching us humility when you, yourself, are *riven* with pride.'

And with that he knelt down, and punched her so hard on the jaw she passed out.

The entire area was silent.

'Call the healers,' he said.

Mayalee sighed audibly.

'Not you,' the captain replied, turning but not facing her. 'You can wait till morning for your part in this mess. I have to go explain this to the King.'

*** 

   By Dr Joe Ireland

Late that evening, Kialessa could not sleep.

Less than a quarter journey away, across the usually placid waters of the widest river of Lenmer'el, thousands if not millions of armed trolls waited.

Just the other day they had attempted to cross that river. They had attempted an invasion. And it was only the gift of the sky dragons that had stopped them. Yet she who had given that gift was nowhere to be seen now, knocked unconscious, and likely chained up in a heap somewhere.

What would stop the troll hoard tomorrow?

Kialessa gave up trying to sleep, and snuck out of her bed. She noticed Allastassia meditating, brushing her hair in long, gentle strokes. Allastassia probably noticed her, but neither spoke to the other.

It was strange to live at the edge of a battle front, where any hour could bring death, and whatever that would mean. Kialessa had to believe there was something watching out for her, giving life, and death, meaning and purpose. Else all this was utter madness.

But waiting to see if the trolls prevailed, and turned everyone into slaves or soil?

It was worth risking death to try and prevent that from happening.

She went up to the king's pavilion, where a commander was drilling a handful of young soldiers. They ignored her.

She heard voices in the nearby tent. Posk was asking

questions again, 'Why is Animas, I mean Annas, the goddess of animals then?'

Piex's voice replied. 'Annas is not just the goddess of animals, but is more accurately considered the goddess of life, and of abundant life. But the prefix "anim-" is from *civit aura*, and refers to "having a soul". The ancients thought only things that move have a soul, and since animals move a lot they are considered to have more abundant life, like the goddess.'

'Fair points,' Posk replied, 'so what's her relationship to Planas then?'

Kialessa was just beginning to lose interest in questions she already knew the answers to when she noticed a small human like-shadow approaching. It was Eclipse.

She looked sad.

Her wounds were healed; there wasn't even a scratch on her clothing.

'I'm leaving,' she announced.

Kialessa's heart skipped a beat. 'No, please,' she begged.

Eclipse did not smile, 'It's clear I'm not wanted here.'

Then Kialessa felt angry. It was not that she wasn't wanted; she was picking a fight with everyone she met! And more often than not, she was losing those fights.

'Eclipse,' Kialessa begged, unable to keep the tears from her eyes.

'No. I've done my duty here. I delivered the message to your king, and I unleashed my mother's prayer to warn

     By Dr Joe Ireland

the trolls. That was all I was required to do. You human's don't want me here. And I don't think … it's wise anymore.'

Kialessa knew there was no stopping her, once she'd made up her mind. But she still wanted to try, 'Eclipse. Don't. Everyone's upset. There's a war going on. Please don't leave. We need you.'

'We? While I wait around to die beside you? Have you seen the number of the trolls? Do you know what that sword of the troll king is capable of? I'm sorry. I'm just… this just isn't me. I have to leave.'

Kialessa didn't know what to say, but Eclipse seemed so resolute. Kialessa nodded, when a movement to the left caught her attention.

It was Bon Sure'e, the captain of the king's guard. He seemed relaxed, his hands in his belt and not on his weapons. Eclipse momentarily tensed, but soon waited for him to speak.

The captain nodded at Kialessa, and then whispered his council quietly in the night, directly to Eclipse, 'You will never find your place in this world until you are honest: about yourself, what you want, and who you are trying to become. For all your foolishness, I hope the fight at least will begin to teach you that.'

She glared at him, but he continued his little life lesson, a surprising piece of wisdom from a usually axe heavy warrior; 'For until you risk presenting your sincere, vulnerable and imperfect self to the judgment of an indifferent world, you will never find a place to belong.'

Eclipse did not answer or argue, but looked angry. Without a sound, she turned into a dragon and curled away into the night sky.

The captain sighed, and walked away towards his barracks.

Kialessa buried her face in her hands. This was a terrible night. In her heart she, too, just wanted to fly away.

But she knew if she did, and the world was destroyed, she would always hate herself for not *trying* to make it, even just a little bit of it, just a little better.

So she decided to stay.

The night grew silent. She could still hear the fires far away, and the night birds calling. But the fire right next to her had lost all sound. The entire area was impossibly silent.

She was about to say something, when she looked up with horror to find the guard knocked unconscious.

Suddenly the ground bulged under Kialessa's feet. She leapt off, and it bulged again. An instant later two troll arms shot from the earth and grabbed her by the legs.

She tried to scream, but no sound came out as though the air was no longer there. It was just like Marchan's silence spell in battle training. The powerful arms wrapped around her, and she only had a moment to reach for her whip. Stretching up as high as she could, she desperately tried to crack it to call for help.

With immeasurable relief she heard it make a solid

crack, sounds of rousing warriors in the nearby tents.

A moment later the powerful arms grabbed her and dragged her, screaming silently, into the unwelcome mound of dirt.

# Dirt And Ultimatum

*One does not **find** where they belong. They **create** it...
and then they create themselves in the image of it.*

*Jindalessa, troll Queensage, ruminations of the lost
wizard page 441.*

The ground closed around her, and for several
moments she was dragged through the earth. An instant
later she found herself bursting from the floor and thrown
into a wooden cage of some sort.

'Kialessa!' a voice called. It was Allastassia.

Kialessa looked around in alarm and fear. She was in a

                    By Dr Joe Ireland

cage, and her captors could apparently run through earth as though it was air. Crosshatched wooden rods marked the door to their prison, which seemed to be placed on a high mound of earth, overlooking some kind of arena or ceremonial grounds. The area was lit with burning torches, which flicked in the faces of hundreds of trolls. They were painted for war, wearing for jewellery the bones of their enemies. They carried their weapons drawn, even their stone daggers had no sheath.

'Kia!' Piex shouted, and he rushed to embrace her. He seemed terrified, and his headband was missing.

A moment later there was a crash as Darrix, followed by his sword and armour still on its nightstand, was thrown into the room via the earth beneath them. He landed on his feet, a feral and dangerous look in his eyes. Kialessa had to pause a moment.

'Kia, is that you?' he said, looking at her eyes.

She nodded.

'Stand down, Darrix. We're all here,' Allastassia told him.

'Me too,' Piex explained. Darrix had terrible night vision, like most humans. Unlike most tae'anaryl, part dragons or fey blooded, it seemed.

Or trolls.

A moment later the earth burst out again, and Posk erupted from it, still wearing his headband. His eyes were molten black, and his teeth filled with a hunk of chainmail armour he'd just torn off some unfortunate troll kidnapper. He looked at them, roared, then cheered.

Then charged the barricade.

'Not now, Posk,' Allastassia tried to tell him, but the young warrior was in a blind rage.

He threw himself again and again at the rods of wood. They creaked and bent, but did not give way. The trolls watching from behind in great interest pulled back at his rage. He then grabbed two rods and began to yank them apart.

The trolls nearby mocked him, then fell silent as the rods bent, and began to splinter.

'Very well then; now,' Allastassia agreed.

Darrix grabbed up Defender, and Piex grabbed some nearby cobwebs for his golden shackles spell. Sharp, dagger like, thorns grew in Allastassia's clenched hands, and Kialessa reached through the shadowrealm for her acid dagger.

'I break you, I break you all!' Posk roared. Trolls cried out in alarm as Posk ripped apart another rod of hardwood, then another. He was working his way rapidly through them. Two trolls threatened him spears, and with almost practiced precision Posk reached through, grabbed the spear tips, and pulled them into the prison with such strength their wielder's faces were smashed into the bars and they were both knocked clean unconscious. A pair of archers took up position, and Piex took them both out with his favourite and oft-used *vivid starclash* spell.

Trolls, the less military sort, fled.

          By Dr Joe Ireland

Kialessa knew this was their chance. They only had a moment before the elite arrived. Screaming, she called for Eclipse. She was their only hope to escape without touching the earth once more, and as good as troll eyesight was, she hoped they would not see a hidden moon dragon and even if they did, that they would have the sense not to anger the sky dragons by attacking one.

Darrix was helping Posk rip up their prison when suddenly the trolls fell silent.

A troll shamaness was approaching, Kialessa immediately recognising her as the one who had spoken with king Dunnkan just the other day. She still looked ready for battle; a bone and feather head dress, carrying her vulture skull staff. She was muttering words to herself, or to Posk. Words which he could never hear. Then Kialessa hear one word that she knew, just a little louder than all the rest, '*Ponere.*'

Posk's eyes instantly returned to normal, and while he kept thrashing against the wood, it did no further damage. He roared, and shook the bars ineffectually.

Then, with a dismissive gesture, the troll shamaness disrupted all the magic in their prison. Allastassia's thorn knives wilted, and Defender seemed to simply switch off. Piex's mage armour shimmered and disappeared, and to her deep disappointment, Kialessa's dagger disappeared back into the shadowrealm.

'Well done, rageling,' the old woman troll said to Posk. 'You have a long way to go before you master your troll fury, but you are powerful indeed. I see your human heritage grants you the power of man's blood. We trolls must make an elixir of the stuff.'

He tried to roar in her face, but she deftly struck her hand through the shattered bars and poked him on his right shoulder. He fell back as though in great pain, and Allastassia rushed to help him.

The shamaness simply laughed. 'You'll have your chance, man blooded. Tomorrow, I'll guess.'

'Let us go,' Allastassia demanded. 'We don't belong here!'

That seemed to touch a nerve in the shamaness. Perhaps she wondered if her armies belonged out here as well. 'Oh, and are you so convinced of that?' she looked at Posk, her glare softened. 'Manblooded half-troll, know this: One does not *find* where they belong. They *create* it... and then they create themselves in the image of it.'

Posk did not reply, but nursed his injured shoulder.

A deep, guttural troll voice roared from the far end of the clearing. The troll shamaness rolled her eyes.

Piex translated, 'He wants to know what's going on. I think it's the warlord... Ki-Taieri.'

The shamaness replied with something forceful and discourteous. And Piex explained, 'She tells him to mind his own business, the prisoners are hers till dawn.'

The troll warlord didn't seem to like that reply, and he stalked over. He was tall, as tall as Darrix's father, only much, much broader. He had the bearing of a warrior;

lean, and muscular. Over his back he had slung his dreaded sabre, still wreathing in green flames.

None impeded his approach, but the shamaness let them all see her displeasure.

'Good,' the troll warlord spoke in Emerellian. Very clear Emerellian too, it could be added, 'You've done well, Jindalessa. You honour the cause.'

Allastassia looked like she might have wanted to say something, but as the shamaness held up her hand, and the enchantress fell silent as though she could not make a sound at all.

The warlord didn't even seem to notice. He bent his head forward toward the prison. Kialessa realised if she had one of those spears she could quite possibly put out one of those eyes right now. Young, unarmed maids were quite the bane of troll warlords, history told.

'I'm going to enjoy this sport,' the warlord told them, leering at them with a spiteful grin. 'Calling for the skydragons again?' he spoke right to Kialessa, and she wondered how he knew. 'They've made their opinion very clear, and it has frightened my people's resolve. But I know this peace will not last, and the humans and their allies wallow in lands that are ours by right of conquest over three hundred years ago. We will reclaim our lands and our rights to govern all your people!'

Darrix stood.

'Oh, you brought the shiny!' the warlord mused.

Darrix replied, he was so courageous, but also so

polite. 'Blood Lord, may I speak?'

'Sure!' the troll warlord shrugged. He was already surrounded by a small force of his black painted elite.

'By voice of your own troll council, our people and yours are at peace until this day. What made you break your oaths, and enter our lands? Why did you attack, forcing the sky dragons to intervene?'

'While human feet walk troll soil, while human hands carve benighted farrows in the mother earth. You disgust and sicken us. We have come to finish the great cause that Father TotoMuru was robbed of three hundred years ago. We have come to seek war with the Great Kingdom of men, and their allies.'

His elite snarled their agreement, which echoed as the message of hate spread throughout the hoard.

All joined it, except, it would seem, the troll shamaness. She stood looking at the soil, an unreadable expression in her eyes.

Then Allastassia spoke, 'But we have not sought war with you. What has any man done, that provokes the troll hoards to war!'

He laughed again, cruel and soft. 'Oh, it's not *only* what you disgusting monsters have done to us that will reignite this glorious war, no, not at all. It's what your people are *going* to do that will finally start this sacred crusade. When they see your skinned and lifeless hides hanging from our banners, they will break their oath to never enter troll lands in order to retrieve your bodies, and when they do,

     By Dr Joe Ireland

when armed soldiers of your people attack innocent warriors on this side of the Broadwaters, it will we clear what kind of **savages** your people are. The **sacred rage** that this betrayal will kindle within all troll hearts will convince them all that there is no safety for us within our own lands until you are no long safe in yours. I will simply stand by while the troll council finally acknowledges all that I have ever known – while the Great Kingdom stands, our warriors will die, our lands are not secure, and our children are not safe. For their protection, for the rights and privileges of government, the Great Kingdom must die.'

No one said anything. That he was mad for power was clear, and nothing but his death or the subjugation of the entire Great Kingdom would stop him.

Kialessa stole a look at the shamaness. She was still silent, looking at the ground. Her shoulders were square, her face determined, but it was clear this female troll did not agree with her warlord. For an instant their eyes met, and in that moment Kialessa saw a steel resolve that frightened her, a cunning patience that equalled the warlord's battle lust pace for pace.

Kialessa did not know how this would play out.

The warlord put his face right up to the bars. 'Goodnight, children of Red King of Lenmer'el. Sleep well; I'll most likely kill you in the morning.'

*You never stand alone. In every moment a million ancestors pray for your survival and success. In deepest darkness, in darkest despair, you are never alone.*
*King Dunnkan, 312 CY.*

Posk, it seemed, was first. Early the next morning thirty or so heavily armed elite troll guards approached their prison. Their leader, the general, watched as they unlocked the door. Two muscled, black painted trolls strolled in, them clasped onto Posk's arms while a forest of spears held Kialessa and his friends back. Before she could do anything they'd dragged Posk out. They clamped an alumium choker onto his neck, and one massive troll, at least three times the size of the rest of them, held the other end of the pole and stopped Posk from getting away. The dragged him into the centre of the arena, and he was forced to kneel.

The troll warlord exited his tent to the cheers of his people. He stood before his throne made of hardwood and ivory, and possibly a dragon's head. The crowd of filthy trolls fell silent, and he address them in his own language.

Piex translated. 'It's whakamātautau – the test.'

'Meaning?' Allastassia asked. Predictably her face and dress were completely clean by this time of the morning.

'I think they're not going to simply kill him.'

Darrix explained, 'They know he's not full human, and want to see if he'd make a better addition to their hoard than a trophy for their banners.'

'He'll never fight for them,' Allastassia told them.

'But he will fight for us, or to protect himself. I suspect that's the play here,' Darrix said. 'Curious. Why are they looking for reasons to kill us when they already have one?'

No one answered.

A moment later the shamaness walked up to Posk and removed his headband of wizardry, the one that allowed him to speak. He tried to stop her, but she was just too quick. A close circle of troll warriors closed around Posk, their shields forming a makeshift battleground. Posk roared with savage fury.

Kialessa found it heartbreaking to see him brought

back low to his animal mind, especially since he was about to go into battle for his life.

The giant troll released the pole from off Posk's still attached alumium collar, and stood back, pole still at the ready. The troll was clearly as thick as two bricks, but it kept any order it was given without thought or question.

Posk roared, his gauntleted knuckles pressed on to the ground just the way they always used to be, especially in combat training. He turned left and right, always watching his cheering, growling captors.

A hurry of drums thundered though the air, and as they stopped a tall troll warrior leapt over the troll's heads to face off against an unarmed Posk. He was painted with red troll paint, and wielded a wooden club embedded with obsidian spearheads. He had an ivory dagger at his hips, and a hardwood shield slung over his back.

'Those are executioner markings!' Piex shouted.

'Posk!' Allastassia shouted, grabbing the bars. Her hands sizzled with arcane power.

An instant later two elite trolls, with a dark shaman, confronted her.

There was no breaking out now.

Darrix grinned, 'Not yet, Alli. Posk is a little bit of a surprise, even to us.'

'But they're trying to kill him,' Allastassia argued, sounding worried. It was understandable; it was Posk versus the entire troll hoard.

The troll ceremonial executioner was stalking around

the arena, soaking up the cheers of the crowd, and giving Posk occasional death stares. With almost no warning he suddenly leapt toward Posk and brought his club down on the ground. Posk scurried quickly out of the way, but it was clearly simply a warning strike. Posk roared, and tried to say something. His expression grew grim as the words failed once more to form from his speechless mind.

Kialessa prayed fervently for her friend.

Again the executioner struck, then again. On the third strike a sliver of obsidian struck true, and grazed Posk all along his left thigh. The crowd cheered.

'Those who do not like violence are advised to look away at this point,' Darrix informed them, sounding not really very concerned.

Posk looked down at the dirt, and the crowd grew silent. When he looked up again, his eyes were pools once more of black.

The executioner only struck once more. Posk leapt towards him and deftly dodged the dangerous weapon mid-air. He struck the executioner on the face, and before he had had the time to fall to the ground, Posk had hit him there at least two more times. The executioner swung his club in close range, and Posk threw it into the night air. He tried to pull his dagger and Posk bit his forearm with such might they could hear the bones splinter from their cage. With nothing but his gauntleted fists Posk struck down again and again at the troll till he stopped moving, permanently.

The hoard was silent.

Then they cheered with excitement, roaring in encouragement. The warlord looked on with mild interest.

Posk looked around. He was not cheering. He looked almost … ashamed.

'His first kill,' Allastassia's voice was sad.

'No,' Darrix disagreed. 'He told me-'

Someone began to rattle some beads. The rattling spread throughout the hoard.  A moment later, to cheers of the crowd, two more troll warriors were thrust into the arena. They were armed with spears, shields, and stone clubs. Their markings were in black mud, and they did not look too enthusiastic to be there.

'Regular soldiers,' Piex explained from the markings and attire.

'Executioners rarely have prisoners put up a serious fight. These are trained to battle.' Darrix explained, seeming quite at ease, and genuinely entertained by the combat.

Posk shouted at them, trying to speak. It tore at Kialessa's heart strings; it seemed he was trying to warn them that they should go back. That they didn't need to fight. That this was not their day to die.

They slowly marched to place him between their spears. Posk pressed his back up against the barricade of shields. He begged them to stand down.

With a nod, the troll soldiers tried to attack at the very same moment. They were fast, almost too fast to see. But

          By Dr Joe Ireland

Posk had already thought through his tactic. He grabbed a shield from the wall of warriors around him and used it to cover one side, the troll who was wielding it almost thrown into the centre of the arena. The first soldier's spear struck the shield with great force, but did not break through the hardwood surface.

Meanwhile Posk was using his other hand to grab the second spear only moments before it could embed itself in his shoulder. Twisting right around he simultaneously pulled the second soldier over – too skilled to let his own spear go. Posk ripped the shield out of the fallen troll's arm, probably dislocating it as he went, and used it to smash the second troll in the face so hard he knocked him out cold.

The first solider hardly had a moment to recover before Posk hit him in the ribs. He stumbled backwards, but the boy was on him in a moment, pummelling him with a flurry of blows that would fell a giant.

The soldier fell to one knee, and Posk stopped hitting him. Posk stood back, and tried to say something once more.

The soldier took Posk's kindness to charge him. He grabbed Posk around the waste and ran forward, probably planning to run him into the ground, or the spears wielded by the trolls at the edge of the arena.

Posk never gave him the chance. He kicked his knees and fell forwards. Posk took the full brunt of the earth underneath their combined weight, but still managed to dig his feet into the soldier's stomach. A moment after they hit the ground Posk pushed up, and sent the troll warrior impossibly high into the night air, and well out of the ring of the arena.

Again the trolls cheered. They were enjoying this immensely.

'I think we can win them,' Allastassia stated, and then drawing enchanters' powers into her breath whispered, 'His name is Posk.'

The chant started slowly, Kialessa could never tell where, but within a breath the entire troll hoard was cheering for the boy. Again and again they thundered his name across the savanna, 'Posk! Posk! Posk!'

By this time the troll warlord looked impressed. He raised a finger, and muttered something to one of his advisors.

A moment later a new troll was seen entering the arena. He bore at his belt three ropes, and at the end of each rope, a feral beast. They looked like dogs, only much hairier, fiercer, and wild.

'Draygon hounds!' Allastassia gasped.

'Natural hunters.' Piex continued, 'We must be in the presence of one of the legendary beast masters.'

'Can't we do something?' Kialessa asked her friends.

'Perhaps, if we-'

'Anything we do will be considered cheating,' Darrix informed them. 'He will just have to go through the same test again, after they're broken our fingers. I highly advise non-interference.'

'They're just going to work him to death anyway,' Allastassia mourned.

'I don't believe so,' Darrix replied. 'My heart tells me this is simply a test, for Posk.'

Kialessa was not so sure. The hunter looked like he'd battled more trolls and men than anyone else there, and his draygon couldn't wait to sink their teeth into anything they could see.

Posk saw him coming, and picked up a soldier's spear. Planting it in the ground behind him, he did the same with the second spear. He backed up against it, making it difficult for the draygon to attack him from behind. Then, to the grim cheering of the crowd, he picked up the executioner's club – being smashed into the ground hadn't seemed to dull its blade in the least.

The beast master approached. He stood there, studying Posk, and unslung a longbow from his shoulder.

'Now that's just unfair,' Allastassia moaned.

'Stand down, this is Posk's fight,' Darrix replied.

But it really was unfair.

The hunter strung his bow, and then pulled out the ropes at his belt. To Kialessa's surprise the draygon did not charge, but immediately began to carefully surround Posk, watching his every move. Posk just stood there, his back to his makeshift barrier, the club held high in his hands.

When the draygon attacked it was in perfect

synchronism with each other, and the hunter's arrow. There was simply no way Posk could have dodged an arrow at that range, and he simply didn't try. Kialessa had not seen it, but Posk was using the club as his only shield, coving his eyes and heart from the arrow. It would have hit him right between his fourth and fifth ribs, but the obsidian embedded club was right there. Dark shards of glass flew from the club and the arrow split, cutting him on his chest but it was barely a scratch.

Yet the draygon knew their craft well. One of them managed to get Posk by his boot and dragged him down, the other two leaping on him in an instant. Posk disappeared for a moment between two furry assailants, and the troll hoard cheered in frantic glee.

A moment later there was a cry of panic from a draygon, and then the other. Their growls of battle became a strangled cry as Posk lifted them up by their throats. The third one tried to pull him down, biting his leg and making it bleed, but Posk lifted his leg up and brought it down on the beast's still open mouth, pinning it to the dirt.

The beast master looked on with bitter anger. He reloaded his bow and Posk threw a struggling draygon at him. It must have taken enormous strength. The beast master dodged it skilfully and let his arrow fly, right into the improved shield that was the hide of his second beast that still remained in Posk's hand.

The beast master gasped with rage and regret.

Pushing off the injured beast at his feet, Posk leapt

     By Dr Joe Ireland

toward the beast master with his gauntleted fists. The troll did not have time to draw another arrow, but pulled instead a large, steel longsword from his waist. Sparks flew as he skilfully parried Posk's deadly assault. The beast master was quick, and Posk still so untrained in comparison. They met each other blow for blow. The entire arena of shields moved away for them. The draygon seemed unwilling to participate by this point.

But Posk was not tiring. He beat the old troll to the edge of the arena where he stumbled on something. Posk took the advantage to bring down both fists on the beast master. It should have ended him, but the lithe troll slipped only a hare's breath from his blow, leapt to his feet in the same skilled move, and stabbed Posk in the back with his dagger.

Allastassia screamed.

Posk swept his arm around, forcing the beast master to leap backwards, preventing him from finishing his task. Posk pulled his hand back from the wound, seeing his own green blood on his hand. The beast master took the chance to regain his breath, dual wielding dagger and sword.

Posk breathed in deeper, and deeper. Again he wiped the blood from his wound.

The beast master looked confused.

Posk took a handful of earth and rubbed it on the wound, and it bled no more. Again and again Posk breathed in deeply, then throwing his head back to the stars, he roared.

Black fire suddenly burst from the ground around Posk, and all nearby leapt away. He menaced up on the beast master, who swung his weapons around in a whirlwind of skilful death. But he simply could not land a telling blow, and those that did healed in instants. Trolls all around were falling back, dropping their weapons; their entire arena edge collapsed.

A moment later Posk stopped the beast master longsword by turning his bare chest into the blow. The wound healed in instants. The beast master, speechless in surprise, forgot to withdraw the weapon which certainly could have caused extra damage. So Posk grabbed the sword with both his gauntlets, and bringing it up into his mouth, bit the sword clean in two.

The beast master knelt in surrender.

The trolls cheered, and chanted his name.

But the fire did not stop around Posk. Leaning down, he picked up the executioner's club, and dragging it along the ground behind him, marched towards the warlord.

Lesser trolls fled. The elite formed a protective wall around their leader, whose momentary fear was soon replaced with undeserved bravado. He drew his black sword and roared a challenge.

Suddenly the ground behind Posk leapt up to form a massive troll hand, and grappled him. He roared, and struggled against it, but it soon hardened and took on the appearance of granite.

　　　　　By Dr Joe Ireland

The warlord roared a protest, but the entire crowd grew completely silent as the troll shamaness entered the arena from the other side. It took Piex to translate the resulting conversation.

"Let him come!" the troll warlord shouted, "if he is so eager for death at my hands!"

"There has been a sign!" the shamaness replied. The hoard fell even more silent at respect to those words.

The warlord slumped on his throne and pushed his blade away from him. It clattered to the ground.

She walked up, and chatted to a still burning Posk. It seemed to be taking a considerable toll on her shamaness powers to hold him there. "Who are you, Posk, half man of Lenmer'el…"

She stood close, staring at his eyes. She sniffed his scent, and looked at him through a stone in her hand.

"Does it matter?" the troll warlord laughed, and his elite with him, "he is dead tonight."

Even from this distance, Kialessa could see the shamaness' eyes fill with wonder, and fear. "By the mischief of the Earth Fire! It is the blood son of the exiled princess TotoAhi!"

The trolls gasped, and look at each other in wonder.

'I haven't heard this story,' Allastassia complained.

Piex answered while trolls muttered in amazement and confusion, 'Rumours of a failed eloping between a troll princess and her guard … almost two decades ago. They were exiled, never heard from again. I wonder if they made it into Lenmer'el? Do you think his parents are still out there?'

'Wouldn't they both be trolls then? How is Posk a half troll?' Kialessa asked.

'No one knows the end of that story, I'm afraid,' Piex admitted.

Trolls muttered, some even dared to bow to Posk. The troll warlord himself stood down from his throne onto the ground, and with a gesture ordered Posk's headband restored. The black fire died around the young half troll, and the hand of stone sunk back into the earth.

'That's some pretty impressive works of faith,' Darrix admitted, looking at the shamaness.

'I wonder what oaths or lore she has with the gods of earth and stone that allow her to do that,' Piex mused.

'Probably stole them from someone,' Allastassia muttered.

Posk stood up tall. A moment one of the soldiers crawled in front of him, trying to reclaim his spear without being noticed. Everyone stared at him.

Piex translated the next conversation as well.

"So," the warlord said, from well without arm's reach. "Son of an exiled princess… how come you to be in the aid of these humans?"

Posk answered, speaking troll moderately well, which was something none of them had realised he could do. "Blood Lord. We have nothing to do with you. Let us go."

He laughed, but grew serious. "I knew your mother.

She was full of temper, that one! It was always wise to respect her wishes… but then again, she was exiled, and I have yet to restore her honour. Now I find she has a whelp? I am not one to suffer an unwelcomed heir."

"Then you have nothing to fear from this one," the shamaness told him. "More than a hundred stand in his way, all more noble, each more trained in our ways. None will stand by the bastard of an exiled princess."

"You speak too soon, shamaness…" the warlord told her. He turned, and looked out at the air. Then he sighed, and looked at his trolls.

Kialessa looked about. There were too many trolls to count, and they all had weapons. But they seemed more to her to be here for the sport of blood, and not for the thrill of death.

'To kill a trespassing human prisoner is one thing,' Darrix smiled a knowing smile, 'But to slay a returning prince?'

Kialessa held her breath.

The troll warlord turned about. "Hear me, hear me, hear me! Drop your sword and draw your skewers, for this evening we feast! For a prince has returned to us! Behold the son of TotoAhi, princess and prophetess, forgiven his mother's trespass! I give you Posk; Black Earthfire and royal half-troll prince!"

Apparently sated for violence, the feast immediately began. Great beasts that could feed twenty trolls were dragged over, and began to bake on enormous spits over blazing fires. Several trolls stepped forward to try and speak to Posk, and probably ask him several questions.

Posk ignored them all in disgust. He marched over to the cage, and demanded to be let in.

'Suffer it to be, for now,' Darrix smiled. 'Learn all you can, you're the man on the inside now, Posk.'

'I'm on the outside, Darrix,' he corrected him.

'He means you're free now to help us,' Allastassia chided.

But the young half troll looked worried. He whispered, 'I'm no prince, Darrix. I want to be in there. If I die, I die with the rest of you.'

Kialessa held his hand, the guards looking on carefully.

Darrix stood up, and reached his hands through the bars to touch Posk's green face. 'It is up to you now, Posk. These are your people. Learn all you can, and, if all else does not work out the way we hope, you alone will be able to tell our parents of our fate. Be brave, be courageous. I saw you burn with dark earth fire, Posk. There is destiny within you that even you are not even aware of.'

Posk looked down, 'I can't even remember how I did that. I hate when they take the headband. Usually I can control the rage but when they take-'

'Oh, dry up, *trollshroom*!' Allastassia chided him. 'Get out there, son of the exiled princess, and live. And bring us some dinner, I'm *starving*!'

Posk glared at her, and she back at him. He gave a wry

     By Dr Joe Ireland

grin, and laughed. Then he went off to join the celebration.

Kialessa shook her head. Apparently Allastassia was one of the few people who had the knack of getting through to Posk as well.

It must have been midnight before he was able to bring meat from the party, but at least they all ate well that day.

# The Visitor

*She does not feel she is worthy of acceptance, and so seeks to find her place among those that will have a hard time accepting her. Either they will accept her, and she will disdain them, or they will reject her and she will feel vindicated in her hatred. There is a narrow window, so very narrow, where kindness may yet find a way to help her choose to accept herself for who she simply is.*

*Jacinthia, high priestess, cited in 'the year in jail'.*

Trolls lay over each other in a poorly organised heap, piled over each other in clumps between her and the warlord's pavilion, weapons still drawn. They looked as bad as always, but she was getting used to the smell. The

     By Dr Joe Ireland

waxing moon's shadows gave the whole area a surreal, calm appearance in the night that denied the desperation of their plight. Winter was coming, and soon her breath would be making clouds in the air. But their cramped prison was surprisingly warm when they huddled together – Posk was like a small oven, and refused to sleep anywhere else, much to the warlord's amusement.

Everyone was asleep, especially the overfed trolls. Kialessa wondered if now was a good time to perhaps escape, but she didn't know how they'd achieve that without making too much noise. The night was so still, Kialessa was beginning to wonder what had awoken her. Then she heard a very soft voice whisper with almost impossible care, 'Kialessa.'

It was Eclipse.

Despite herself, Kialessa almost leapt up to see where the voice had come from.

Eclipse held her hand up for silence. She was standing right there, in the prison with them.

Kialessa barely stifled her surprised gasp.

Without making a sound Eclipse knelt down to whisper to her, and Kialessa snuggled into the shadows nearby. She thought it was absolutely vital that they didn't know Eclipse was here – no need to give them another prisoner. How she had gotten here was another secret, had the wizard teleported her?

'My friend,' Kialessa whispered, 'Go, go, you can't stay here.'

Eclipse looked unimpressed, then she looked sad. 'I saw them take you. I'm so sorry Kialessa – I **knew** I should have stayed! I'm so, so sorry!'

'No, no, don't be, it's not your fault,' Kialessa wished she could make her friend believe her.

'King Dunnkan sent me,' Eclipse replied. 'Is what they say true? Are the trolls really planning to use you all to bait the kingdom of Lenmer'el into trespassing on troll lands?'

'Yes,' Kialessa admitted.

'Monsters; I wish I could destroy them all,' Eclipse muttered.

Kialessa was grateful Eclipse didn't just leap out there and start attacking them. Perhaps her lessons at the hands of the elite were paying off. At least she didn't seem to have a burning need to prove her draconic superiority at all costs right now.

It was also good to know that the king knew their situation. 'How did you know?' Kialessa asked.

'The priestess was sent a vision by a gem of Mya as soon as it happened. They know,' Eclipse grinned.

'So what do we do?' Kialessa asked.

Eclipse sighed, 'No one knows. The sky dragons feel they have done their part, they will not intervene further. Your king knows he cannot cross into troll lands to save you without starting a war – we know it's exactly what the troll king is hoping. At best you must hope for escape, for I do not yet have sufficient gifts to carry you all.'

Kialessa nodded, and held her hand. It was still good



By Dr Joe Ireland

to see her.

'Here,' Eclipse said with a gentle smile. She seemed to be grateful that she could be helping. 'Your king bids you a few gifts for your trial. For Darrix, this collar. I think it is for a dog, I do not see what good it can do! And for Allastassia, this ring. It has a blue lace agate but no current enchantment; I hope she knows what it is for. For Posk, a common rock, obsidian I think. Curious no? To Piex, he gives a tuning fork. It is one of the oddest gifts to a prisoner I have ever seen, but then again, he is a wizard so perhaps there is wisdom. And for you, perhaps the most useless gift of all; scripture.'

Kialessa's heart leapt with joy. Scripture! Comfort and solace of a higher purpose and being in all this trial? This was not only a precious gift; it was one only a true friend would know she would appreciate right now.

Eclipse handed her the small, leather-bound book. It was so slight she could fit it into her armour and almost none would know it was there. There was a warmth and comfort in the book that Kialessa already drew strength from.

Eclipse smiled. Perhaps the claim that it was all "useless" was just a jibe, for even she could see it was not useless to her.

But they were strange gifts.

But then Kialessa realised something, if the wizard had teleported her in there, how was she going to get home?

Eclipse must have sensed something from her

expression. 'Oh, don't worry about me Kialessa. I might not have the gifts to take you from here, but I am not bound by these walls, or any.'

Kialessa was curious. Eclipse didn't look like she was about to break out of the jail just yet, what did she mean?

'A gift,' Eclipse smiled, 'from my murderous father...' and with that, Eclipse turned into a *ghost*.

It was the strangest thing Kialessa had ever seen, and she almost cried out in alarm. Without any apparent effort Eclipse became see-through and insubstantial. Then, with a silent bow of goodbye, she drifted through the floor and flew out through the earth.

Kialessa was musing on the strangeness of the scene till a pale dawn drifted over the morning horizon. She wasted no time, but gave the gifts to her friends as soon as it was light enough for them to see.

It was comfort to know the army was just over the river praying for them.

       By Dr Joe Ireland

# And All Troll Fealty

*"Lies! What must I do to prove I am a worthy king!" – Ki-Tieri, high king of all trolls, 313CY*

*"You would have me tell you again? You must be willing to do so much more than die to protect your people; you must be willing to **live** for them! You must swear to protect them and honour your oath by the things you choose to do. You must avenge them of every injustice, and see they live in peace… And you must be willing to sacrifice your own ends to see your that people live in prosperity and peace." – Jindalessa.*

'Check this out!' Posk grinned. He was holding out his arm. 'They got these needles dipped in, I don't know. And just put them in there, it's a picture! Look!'

It was a tattoo, right on his bicep muscle. They'd had to learn all about muscles and nerves at the college in case they needed to stab someone, though Kialessa had never really realised how important it might be one day. College was always very practical like that – even the noble children had been taught how to cook and set a tent.

'It's your mother's national symbol,' Piex explained. 'And these markings here represent your acceptance as a man, because you killed someone yesterday.'

Posk looked a bit glum. 'So that's what you have to do to belong here?' he muttered, looking thoughtful. '*Awful…* but I hardly even remember it…'

'Well, it means you're officially one of them,' Allastassia announced.

'Good news for you if the rest of us die,' Piex muttered.

'We'll I will surely die if you don't **get us some breakfast**, Posk!'

'Right, yeah, that,' Posk nodded, and scurried off to see what he could find, not at all protesting Allastassia's shouting. It was a great kindness; they might eat at all today otherwise.

'So,' Allastassia spoke, since they dare not mention their visitor that night. 'Posk is royalty. I would have never guessed.'

Darrix grinned, 'You've seen him fight, all year, Ali. Was there never a clue?'

'Like you could tell,' Allastassia jeered.

'It was one of the more popular theories among us

boys,' Darrix claimed. 'Overpowered half troll of mysterious parentage? The odds were always in his favour.'

'I can confirm this information,' Piex said, staring out at the sloven trolls in the early morning, probably now reading something in his imagination.

'Well, I'll be,' Allastassia mused, saying no more.

'Who do you think will be tested next?' Kialessa asked.

No one answered.

'It hardly seems like we've had enough time, does it, Kia.' Allastassia wondered out loud. 'All this time preparing to fight for our lives, and now here we are… it's hard to know what to do.'

'I've been analysing the fight,' Darrix told them. 'Posk showed us something. He didn't kill everyone he faced, and the trolls seem to respect that. Something is going on here… do you notice the way that shamaness disrespects her leader?'

They looked at each other. Everyone had noticed.

'We need to know what's **really** going on here,' Allastassia announced.

A moment later a small procession quickly gathered everyone's attention. Trolls cheered.

'What is this?' Allastassia wondered.

The cheering grew. Kialessa scurried up the wooden bars to look out at the gathering. Soon she noticed that there was something moving through the crowd.

'They say it's the blood spear,' Piex said.

'Go on,' Darrix said, encouraging him to explain. They had all climbed the bars and were all craning their necks to see above the excited throng.

'During the troll uprising three hundred years ago, TotoMuru, the first troll king of all five lands, was known as the "blood lord" as he was thus named for good reason – that spear. With it, he was undefeatable.'

'How do you mean?' Kialessa asked, now the strange bier was out of sight.

Piex fidgeted, the way he was when he was nervous. 'Well, it works similar … you know the rod of the King of Lenmer'el?' he asked.

She nodded. It was a black rod with a diamond sphere, and no one was supposed to be able to touch it. No one, except the king and his divinely appointed protector; the steward. And, apparently, her, though no one still had a reason why. It held within the promise of every person in the land to protect the king and kingdom. And that much desire was a very powerful thing in a world full of magic.

'Well,' Piex continued, 'it works in a similar science. It contains the promise of all the five troll nations and every troll to protect and honour their one king. But, unlike the rod of Lenmer'el it goes a quite a bit further. It asks total obeisance; it asks for everything. From it the blood lord could draw their strength, their magic… even their ability to heal. They say there was nothing like it. He could punch through solid stone, tear apart even magical barriers. Even if they cut off his arm, it just grew right back…'

                    By Dr Joe Ireland

'Then this does not bode well for the war,' Darrix admitted.

'Ya think?' Allastassia muttered.

'The only way to defeat him, or so they thought, was to kill every troll who had sworn fealty to the spear. It was set to be a long and terrible war. And it would have been as well, except for the maidservant.'

'The maidservant!' Kialessa knew this story.

Darrix nodded, but told it anyway, 'One of the blood lord's many servants. She was quite young, it is said. Imagine the war: The Great Kingdom was in tatters, but it was fighting back, under Emerel; the kingdoms were winning again. The troll council convened and all voted unanimously to end the conflict. It is said even *they* had had their fill of war. They felt the message had been given to allow the trolls to live in dignity and peace... but it was not enough for TotoMuru. He had already declared the death oath – that he and his chosen would continue fighting until all their enemies were slain, or death took them. Thus the gods would choose the moment that the battle must end. And not trolls, or humans, nor any other ally or event could change his mind. Yet the humans had new tactics, and had new weapons that put at defiance the troll hoards. The trolls were strong, but they were beginning to lose. But the blood lord had sworn his oath.'

Allastassia continued the story, 'In the end, it was not sword nor strength, not tactics nor skyfire that intervened. It was a single troll serving maid. She was hurt that her brother had died, and begged TotoMuru to let her return to bury him in his native lands. But he forbade it, demanding all return to finish the war. He treated her harshly, striking her to the ground for her weakness. All feared TotoMuru had no end for his war; that he would continue until all was ash or dust. Thus, that evening after the great council, she stole into his tent at night, and while the spear was still in his grasp, nailed a tent peg through his temple with such strength it buried deep into the ground – yet he did not heal, but died. Then, with a scream, she confessed her crime.'

Piex then spoke, 'In that instant TotoMuru's battle lust fell from their hearts, and all trolls knew the gods had, indeed, stepped in to declare the war was over. As the troll council met that dawn, the white dawn, the war officially ended and they restored all lands back to the Great Kingdom in return for eternal peace in their own. It was the last time the troll council ever convened in lands other than their own.'

'Didn't they try to raise him?' Kialessa had always wondered.

'Yes, of course,' Darrix answered. 'But his spirit did not heed the call. Perhaps he considered this his answer, and knew in his own heart the war had ended, and his leadership was no longer of service to his people's highest good.'

'Or perhaps,' Kialessa offered, 'his death was too traumatic for his spirit to return?'

     By Dr Joe Ireland

'Unlikely,' Piex argued. 'His whole life knew violence. No, I like the elven theory – that he lives on even now, trapped as a spirit of savagery and war. He's still here, manifested in the troll hatred of humanity that compels them to war even now.'

Kialessa looked at the trolls. They seemed … happy. Celebrating the spear. But it was not a savage glee, at least, not for most of them. Ki-Taieri and his black trolls, well, they were a different matter entirely.

'Look at them all,' Allastassia argued. 'Brutal, cruel, savage. They have all come for war, and while it means the end of Lenmer'el, I hope I live to see the day the Great Kingdom kills every last one of them!'

But now that Posk was one of them, Kialessa wasn't sure where that war would end, and who by the end of it would still be considered a dear friend.

The bier carrying the legendary weapon moved into her sight again, to the foot of the mound that led to Ki-Taieri's pavilion. The spear itself did not seem too frightening. It had a dark hardwood shaft, tipped with a green obsidian head. A handful of objects were strung on a leather cord by the spear's head; they looked like gems or crystals, it was difficult to tell. The spear rested on a blue granite stone bier that six strong trolls carried. The other troll cheered or bowed, some even shed tears at this totem of their unity and strength.

Darrix whispered to her, 'It is said the Blood Lord started the war in retribution to the slavery and murder of trolls at the hands of the humans and their allies. We don't like to speak of it, but it is true. Trolls were once treated as human property on our side of the river; I am so ashamed to say.'

Just in that moment Kialessa's eyes were drawn towards the shamaness. She stood at the foot of the stairs leading to the pavilion. She looked inspired, enchanted. But her expression was grim, her jaw set tight.

Kialessa lost sight of the spear momentarily as it was carried towards the warlord's pavilion. A moment later he emerged in full battle gear, to the raucous cheers of his warriors. He held his fists up high, and cheered out loud, roaring words of battle.

Piex stood by her, 'He invokes the spirits of the ancient warriors bless them on this day the human empire begins to fall… I guess they have been waiting for the spear to arrive, he thinks it will grant him easy victory.'

'If what I have heard is true, it seems he may be right,' Kialessa muttered.

The crowd grew silent, and the warlord began to descend his stone steps towards the spear, hand outstretched.

Suddenly a solemn fear settled on the entire area. Time seemed to slow down, and an unnatural silence filled their hearts. Somewhere next to her imagination Kialessa heard the echoed beating of distant troll drums, the war chants of a people oppressed. Destiny seemed to hold its very breath.

    By Dr Joe Ireland

The warlord roared, and fell backwards.

Piex translated, "Why does it not let me touch it?!" he shouted at his priestess.

She laughed, "As I told you, the totem of the Blood Lord does not yet accept you as the King and Protector of all five nations. You have not yet proven your worth."

"Lies! What must I do to prove I am a worthy king!"

The shamaness was silent a moment. She walked to the bier, and ran a hand along the stone. "You would have me tell you again? You must be willing to do so much more than die to protect your people; you must be willing to *live* for them! You must swear to protect them and honour your oath by the things you choose to do. You must avenge them of every injustice, and see they live in peace."

"Then I am already worthy!" He shouted, yet to Kialessa's ears he was beginning to sound like a spoiled prince.

The shamaness smiled, "And, need I explain, you must be willing to sacrifice your own ends to see that your people live in prosperity and peace. You must do them justice, and kindness, at all times."

The warlord roared, and defied her. "I am Lord by right of blood and conquest of all five tribes! I have brought you all here to defeat our common enemy! I am worthy to wield the spear of the Blood Lord!" Piex probably didn't need to translate that bit, but he did anyway.

With that, the warlord leapt forward in an attempt to

lay the hand on the spear. Deep red fire, the colour of ochre, exploded around the stone. The troll warlord fell back, nursing charred skin.

Trolls muttered their surprise and, perhaps, disappointment.

Kialessa could not believe it, but the troll shamaness actually laughed. Not a deep mockery, but a gentle chastisement. "Mighty warlord, king of the five tribes. Your time has not yet come. So until it does, and if it does, I will hold on to this for you."

And with that, the shamaness reach over and picked up the spear without harm, slung it over her shoulder, and began to walk away with it.

Trolls leapt out of her way.

The warlord looked confused, but recovered quickly, "Behold, my wife and high priestess, you may bear the mighty spear of the Blood Lord for me until I require it. Give honour; give honour to the bearer of the blood spear!"

Trolls took up the chanting quickly, afraid of the warlord, or believing his words without question. The shamaness sniffed in derision at their fawning. It seemed she needed no king's permission to bear whatever burden she chose.

Allastassia actually laughed out loud at the scene.

'Who is that?' Darrix asked.

Kialessa looked to where he was pointing. A troll, one of their sleepy guards, was kneeling before the warlord

                    By Dr Joe Ireland

and whispering to him frantically. He pointed towards the prison, in particular, he pointed at Kialessa.

A sickening feeling imbedded itself in her stomach as the already very angry warlord glared in their direction.

'Ahh, folks,' Kialessa roused the others.

The warlord began to make his way toward with a quick, determined pace. All the troll's attention turned their way.

Allastassia armed herself with lightning, and Darrix drew Defender.

The warlord was there in only a moment, his dread blade drawn. With a single hand he tore the entire prison door away, without any apparent effort. They might have escaped, but the forest of a hundred troll spears prevented them from going anywhere. Faster then she could react, he reached in and grabbed Kilaessa by the neck. She heard a crackle of electricity from Allastassia, but could do nothing as he pulled her from their cage and threw her to the ground.

'I never liked tae'anaryn,' the troll lord hissed in their only common language, and time seemed to pause. Nobody moved as Kialessa awaited her fate, crouched on the ground before the king of all trolls, her dagger only a thought away yet even it seemed a toothpick in comparison to the weapon he held in one hand. 'There aren't any tae'anaryn among trolls for we kill them the day they are born. Why you are suffered to live among the humans I may never know, but my shamaness divined that you would be effective bait. And when I saw you riding that sky dragon I knew it would be fitting punishment for their interference in my war to see your skinless hide strung up this side of the river. But now this, what is this I hear? Are you friend, also, to the Fell dragons? I know you tae'anaryl must walk the thin line between good and evil, but to mediate between the dragon servants of Neth,' he spat,' and the dragons of the white dawn? You are too much trouble little one. Get out.'

Kialessa didn't move. She wasn't sure what she'd just heard. Did he just let her go?

'**Get out**, little one. I grant you your life.'

'Why?' she had to know.

He laughed in soft mockery. 'We have enough trouble now that the Sky dragons have shown their displeasure. To invoke the wrath of their mortal enemies, the Fell, also? We cannot afford that many enemies even at this time. Get out.'

Kialessa looked over at her friends. Their faces were a mix of horror, and relief.

*Go*, Allastassia mouthed.

It seemed so unfair, so very wrong to leave her friends to their underserved fate alone. To have them face the horror of abduction and death.

'No,' she told the king.

His grip tightened on his black sword. She saw it now, green glowing runes of power along the blade, green fire flowing down the central split and running along the

         By Dr Joe Ireland

ground. Whatever power Kialessa held in her dwarven blade, she knew it was eclipsed by the might of this kingly weapon.

Then the troll king laughed, and his trolls soon with him.

'Get...' he roared, and his enormous hand wrapped around her waist, '...out!'

And with that, he flung her a dozen paces out of the area. She flew through the air in an uncontrolled plummet, and despite trying to turn into a controlled roll as she'd been taught in the circus, rolled a dozen times before she stopped. She hit hard, but was still grateful to see he'd somehow managed to land her right at the river's edge – knee deep in soft, rich, mud. It hurt, but she was all right.

She could still hear the trolls laughing over the hill, and tears sprung to her eyes. Tears of fear for her friends, or perhaps in relief for herself. She turned and watched the burning torches of the army of Lenmer'el across the river, even during the day. It brought her deep comfort. Just over the deep grass and rolling hill, a single bright gold and blue pennant shone its defiance in the sun.

Kialessa stood, and tried to find some way to cross. The rope was still strung up between the banks, and the barges on opposite sides. She would just have to walk it.

A moment later a dark flash of movement crossed her vision. It seemed a snake with wings flew from the king's land, and it took Kialessa only a breath to realise it was Eclipse. The dragon made her way cautiously toward her, keeping low in the sky. Without a sound she approached, and daring not to touch the riverbank slid instead right into the water.

Kialessa gratefully waded out into the water to hug her friend.

'Not yet, get on, get on!' Eclipse whispered.

Kialessa held back her sobs as she climbed on, not even thinking to wipe away the mud.

Eclipse swam quickly out into the middle of the river, her powerful tail pushing her on. It took a mighty effort to get airborne, but beating her wings and kicking the water she somehow managed to lift them both into the air.

From the vantage point Kialessa could clearly see her king's camp, its large blue and golden pavilion set out on the field at the same level as all the soldiers' tents. The war wagons were converted into heavy artillery, and wall of pickets surrounding the soldiers. It was a hastily constructed defence set on the largest hill in the area. It was a formidable protection, but it would never last very long against a ten thousand times their number of trolls just across the river.

Kialessa turned, and watched the troll hoard. It was difficult to see the warlord's tent, and the arena, but she knew where they were. Beyond them, campfires glowed in the morning, surrounded by dozens if not hundreds of trolls. And those campfires continued far away, as far as she could see, stretching right to the horizon.

'Indeed,' Eclipse said dryly. 'ALL the trolls have come

to war. All they lack… is an excuse.'

***

It seemed like only a moment later that Eclipse rode down through the morning light and brought Kialessa back to her king.

He rushed to greet her, with his personal bodyguard and the other elite. Some even cheered to see her, calling out her name, and the name of her dragon. Kialessa noticed the captain of the king's guard nod at Eclipse, and she nodded back.

'Thank you for coming to get me,' Kialessa said to Eclipse, 'I know that was very brave.'

'The priestess sent me,' she huffed.

The next moment King Dunnkan reached up and pulled her from the dragon's back. His eyes were full of tears, which might have explained why Kialessa burst into sobbing. He knelt on the floor, hugging her.

'Are you all right?' he asked her.

She really couldn't answer him right away, but pressing back her sobs, she tried. 'They took us through the earth, and kept us … and keeping us in a cave that overlooks the warlord's arena. They made Posk fight.'

The wizard gasped, and soldiers murmured.

'It's all right,' Kialessa explained, 'he won.'

They nodded their agreement.

'Then he burst into black flames, almost took on their

warlord single handed, and then the warlord's priestess declared Posk to be the son of an exiled troll princess.'

The soldiers sounded impressed.

'That does explain a few things,' the steward muttered.

'What of the others, Kialessa,' her king asked.

Her heart knotted with pain. 'The warlord intends to make them fight, and hopes they die. Then will use their… bodies to try and make you cross the Broadwaters.'

'And then,' the dwarven priestess of the king said, 'the warlord will use this as an excuse to "prove" we cannot keep our oaths, that we intend him harm, and that we sent a military force into their lands. He will use that as a pretext to invade.'

'I know,' Kialessa could barely say the words.

The king hugged her again, as though he wished he could keep such words from entering her ears. But they would.

'What mad tradition have we of bringing children into war!' he whispered.

'Better to die here,' Kialessa said.

'Making a difference,' the captain agreed.

King Dunnkan held her back from him. 'Well, have you anything else to tell us?'

Kialessa wondered, thinking about what she'd seen. 'There's a … his high priestess does not support him. I don't think … I think most of the trolls don't actually want a war, just the warlord and his elite.'

It looked like the soldiers did not believe her, but the



By Dr Joe Ireland

king looked relieved. He looked at his priestess, and she nodded.

'Then we wait?' the wizard asked.

The king thought about it for a moment. 'I have a clever idea, an inkling, if you will Kialessa? Come with me, I have a little errand for you.'

# He Who Sings

*You don't understand. Sometimes those raised harshly come to believe deep in their souls that they are not worthy of any kindness, or love. Then, when they are shown it, and not matter how much they are shown it, they rejected it, unconsciously at first – refusing to believe a compliment, refusing to accept the offer of a kind deed, simply because it makes them feel uncomfortable. They cannot believe they are worthy of such kindness. Eventually they, like all beings, will seek to find a place more comfortable, more in tune with what they believe they are worth; even if such places are very, very dark. Thus they work their own way towards regret, and are almost never in a way forced there.*

*Jacinthia, high priestess, in 'The year in jail'.*

Eclipse landed, without any apparent fear, right in the

                    By Dr Joe Ireland

middle of the warlord's arena. The troll elite had drawn their weapons, but they did not look afraid. Kialessa jumped down from her back, the chest of treasure in her hands, even as Eclipse turned back into a young girl.

The trolls might not have been afraid, but they certainly gave them their attention.

A moment later Ki-Taieri, his wife by his side, exited his tent. 'Oh, the little tae'anaryn returns, and with her dragon, child of the Sky,' he mocked.

Eclipse seethed with anger. A week ago, she would have attacked them all for such insult. Today, she was a little wiser.

Kialessa curtsied her best, and spoke in the only language she knew, 'Mighty king of all trolls. I bring an offering of the people of Lenmer'el, to pay for peace and the lives of my friends. We beg you to reconsider the need for war, and invite you and any you so desire come over the river and discuss in peace-'

"Peace?" the warlord roared. 'All human lands belong to US.' His elite cheered, but it was clear to Kialessa's eyes not that the other trolls did not support this claim, either that, or they did not speak Emerellian. The warlord turned to his general, 'Take these trinkets and put them with the others. They are a poor offering for the King of trolls.'

'You will find,' Eclipse walked forward without a trace of fear, her bored voice now tinged with a threat. 'That those trinkets, though small, are of immense worth to you trolls. Diamonds, and gems of such skill that you trolls have never mastered. And a vial of men's blood, freely given.'

The warlord gripped his general's arm, and ripped the lid off the chest. He held out the vial, and his people cheered. He then held it out to his wife, who with some grim acknowledgement took it away.

Then he laughed, 'I claim this treasure as the right of all trolls anyway!'

'Thieves!' Eclipse accused him, and the arena fell silent.

'Then,' the warlord corrected himself, 'as payment for you lives. As permission to speak to me today. If you want to pay us out for war, yield to us all those lands and golds which are ours.'

'And have the humans live as slaves?' Eclipse accused him.

'It would only be fair,' the warlord shrugged. 'But you'll find us much less savage than the humans were to us three hundred years ago. No, the humans may live as one, with us, among us. As equals.'

'I do not believe your word this day, not for one moment,' Eclipse said darkly, a sentiment Kialessa felt she deeply agreed with. The warlord would kill every human that did not submit to slavery, this was clear.

'Go your own way,' he commanded, 'I give you your lives this day in troll lands for these… trinkets.'

'Come,' Eclipse offered to Kialessa.

But Kialessa had heard the warlord's careless words. 'No, thank you. I think I will stay.'

    By Dr Joe Ireland

He turned, and looked surprised.

Kialessa curtsied, and went to sit over by her friends, just outside the prison cage. They reached out and held hands.

The troll king, and his people, laughed.

Eclipse looked over at her.

'We… would be honoured to have you accompany us, as much as it suits you,' Darrix offered.

Eclipse said nothing, but walking away glanced over at Kialessa with a sad look. It was as if a part of her wanted to stay, and another part of her wanted to get away. Kialessa wasn't sure what Eclipse wanted. But walking out of sight over the hill, she turned into her dragon form, and flew across the river.

'She seeks her own place,' Posk decided.

***

The party was lighter this time; the trolls seemed to be in a more peaceful mood. Several women danced and sang, ignored by their warlord. He was eating quietly with several of his commanders and fellow warriors. They were the elite, it was clear. They sat, eating with their fingers, pulling tufts of baked meat from the animal they had cooked. They sat close to each other, rubbing shoulders and occasionally shoving each other as they laughed. A new plate of meat was brought, and Kialessa watched as the warlord and his general reached at the same time. With a laugh, the warlord indicated the general should eat first, who with a polite grunt, did just so.

'How they disgust me,' Allastassia said.  'Eating with their fingers.'

'It's the troll way,' Piex replied.

'Their way is disgusting, lawless, filthy. No wonder they were almost wiped out in the first war. I hate trolls.'

They watched them in silence.

'Surely we trolls are not all that bad,' Posk muttered from outside their cage. He'd been helping Kialessa bring the others what food they could.

Allastassia huffed, and gave him a small smile.

'I don't think trolls are disgusting,' Kialessa said. 'They are different to us, it is true. But they are still very polite, in their own way.'

'They cover their hands with ash and dirt before they eat!' Allastassia protested.

'And we cover ours with water,' Darrix agreed with Kialessa. 'I don't know if some dirt is cleaner than others, but they are very careful to, um… clean up, in their own way.'

'They eat with their hands, sitting on the floor!' Allastassia's lip curled in disgust.

'And they take turns, and share everything,' Kialessa argued.

Allastassia was quite for a moment, 'And they're going to kill every one of us.'

Suddenly one of the troll generals that kept the prison

　　　　By Dr Joe Ireland

yelled out to the prison guards.

'Oh-oh,' Posk muttered.

It only took a gesture from the warlord, but a moment later a dozen trolls surged against their prison, tore open the recently repaired door, and laid hands on the first person they could.

Piex was dragged out, despite Allastassia's screams and pleading.

Kialessa heard him mutter as they dragged him by, 'I guess I die today.'

She had nothing to say to that, but prayed fervently in her heart.

Strong trolls held Kialessa and Posk down, but allowed them to sit where they could clearly see what was happening. Piex was dragged in front of the warlord, who hadn't moved from his earthen dinner table. His wife had arrived, and stood at the far side.

Piex was pale, and trembling. Kialessa watched as he fiddled with something in his lap. She strained to look, expecting to see him getting ready to use a scroll or some other kind of magical ingredient. But it was the silver glint of the turning fork that caught her eye.

The warlord spoke in Emerellian, 'Little dragon boy. You are sure to be poor sport for the least of my warriors.'

The trolls laughed.

'And if we had need of meat we still would have no use for those twig arms!'

The trolls laughed harder, but not cruelly.

The warlord's wife waited with a small grin on her face. Kialessa wasn't sure if she liked the "joke", or if she knew something nobody else did. That she was a priestess to match the might of Jacinthia was already clearly established.

The warlord sighed. 'And I'm not inclined to pick a fight with star dragons. That they leave you to rot and waste away among humans is clear, but someone up there might have some feeling for you. So, part dragon; plead for your life.'

For a long moment, Piex just sat there. He looked nervous, terrified.

But he did not speak.

The moments continued to pass as the silence grew.

'Well!' the warlord roared.

Piex's body shook with fright.

Suddenly a soft, whispered note from a tuning fork hummed through the arena, bringing gentle silence to complete stillness.

And Piex started to sing.

It was a simple tune Kialessa instantly recognised. His 'performance piece', the lullaby of the air element that instructed the young in the rudiments of their sacred, ancient language.

Trolls began to snicker, and the priestess snorted them to silence with a clenching of her fist. Even the warlord did not contest that gesture.

Yet as her fist released, she passed two fingers in the

direction of Piex.

'She blesses him!' Posk whispered.

Piex's song continued in the abject silence of the lands by the Broadwaters. Even the insects fell silent, the only accompaniment the gentle flowing of the mighty river. Clouds of air formed in the magic around the young wizard; runes, and letters of a language none but he knew. Soon, the humming of the fork changed pitch, and Kialessa realised he was using it to form a clever countermelody to harmonise with his song. A reverent stillness settled on the area, and the air seemed to become … lighter, softer. The music was, once more, simple, beautiful, and the trolls listened with intense respect.

Kialessa watched over at the warlord. He was mesmerized with the song.

Soon, the music ended, and to Kialessa's unspeakable amazement a single tear flowed down the warlord's cheek.

Kialessa watched over at Allastassia, wanting to say something like, "See, they do have hearts," but quickly realised she did not need to as the enchantress looked over with wonder.

The music ended, yet none dared break the silence.

The warlord breathed in deeply, and it seemed to break the mood. Trolls were grunting their approval, many nodded in Piex's direction as though he had won some kind of epic battle, and had gained their undying respect.

Soon, a handful of curiously small trolls pressed their way through the group to kneel at the warlord's table. They were very short, with large heads, oversized hands, and bent postures. They weren't dressed like the other trolls. They had robes, and vests filled with what looked like quills and parchments. One of them was even carrying a book almost as big as he was.

Their leader, an old bespectacled troll, spoke first. His voice stuttering out Emerellian from nervous lips, 'Ki-Taieri, please. If we may humbly beg your magnanimous indulgence! This draconling is of use to us! He is as we are, a *scholar*. If we could claim him, for a few days perhaps? We could teach him of our ways, and learn from him this script-'

'Pah,' the warlord shrugged, 'I have no taste for elven-

'

'Air speech, my lord,' the scholar corrected, them seemed to hate himself even more for interrupting his king. 'It's air speech… much more advanced, the language of the elemental beings of the air. The engravings on the ancient tomb of -'

'Enough!' the warlord ordered with a wave of his hand. 'Take him. He wouldn't even be a snack.'

The troll warriors laughed, and the little troll ran to Piex. With both hands open, he offered to help the young wizard to rise, indicating they needed to hurry. The other scholars looked very nervous, and out of place amongst the warriors.

 By Dr Joe Ireland

'Do we look so vile to your eyes, enchantress!' A voice demanded near Kialessa. It was the troll shamaness.

Allastassia did not answer, 'What they are going to do with him?'

The shamaness huffed, 'Teach him, I fear. Tell him things our enemies should not know, and if he has any wisdom he will not be too keen to tell them the secrets he knows.'

'Then we are doomed,' Posk mourned.

With a wave the shamaness ordered the guards release Kialessa and Posk. Without a pause Posk ran after Piex.

The shamaness indicated Kialessa should join her, and no trolls impeded them. She returned to the prison, and spoke right to Allastassia. 'You will be next, fire haired enchantress. I hope that boy has taught you something about our people that you might have never learned on your own. We were never the savages your soldiers would have us believe we are, nor...' she added as an afterthought, 'as my husband would have us behave.' Turning to leave she cast words over her shoulder, 'Prepare yourself.'

Allastassia clutched the bars with dark determination.

Darrix went to put his arm around her, but she shoved him off.

'Let's get this over with now,' she whispered, dark green lightning rippling from her fingertips. She set her jaw tight, and glared at the warlord.

Kialessa saw him glance over, but he did not stop his

meal.

Allastassia would have to wait, and the party was only just starting.

                    By Dr Joe Ireland

## She Who Dances

*Be yourself – everyone else is already taken.*
*Humdug, dwarf scholar.*

Midnight approached under Lumos' waxing crescent and the trolls were getting wild, their celebrations growing more and more riotous as the night wore on. Then someone brought out the large set of drums, and the party really kicked in.

Posk hadn't been by to feed them, which meant Kialessa had to sneak up and grab some food from the trolls. They tried to stop her, but she'd remembered Piex's teachings and fought them away. They were strong, and quick. But she was faster, and smaller. Soon she had enough for Allastassia and Darrix to get by, but things were getting loud.

Kialessa pressed her fists to her sensitive ears, leaning against the bars where her friends still waited. Fifty trolls kept banging the ground with their feet as they danced in the centre of the arena. It looked like it might have been lots of fun, if it wasn't so loud.

Then a young troll woman left the dance floor, tears in her eyes. Some young troll man grabbed her hand, trying to tell her something. She paused, but then fled weeping. He watched her leave. Then he glanced in Kialessa's direction, sneered, then walked away in the opposite direction.

'I guess some things are the same *anywhere*,' Allastassia muttered.

A roar went up from the dancefloor. Kialessa looked over, a soft fear settling on her stomach: Allastassia's time had arrived.

The music died down, and the troll dance hoard parted to reveal Ki-Taieri in the middle of the dance arena. He was leaning heavily on a pair of other trolls. A clay bottle was in his hand, and he took a swig from it, shouting in their language. They roared a cheer in his reply.

Then the warlord seemed to sober up for a moment. 'Bring out the fire-haired female!'

The hoard was on them in an instant. Allastassia was about to be dragged out when she unleashed some

          By Dr Joe Ireland

warning lighting at the trolls. They stood back, and with unruffled dignity, Allastassia stalked out from among them to face the warlord alone. The trolls growled at her with fetid breath, but she showed no fear.

The warlord cheered with grin, and almost looked impressed. Armed with only his bottle and clearly enjoying himself he welcomed her into the arena with a wave of his hand.

Allastassia stood, ready for a fight.

He laughed, and circling her pulled a lock of her hair and sniffed it.

She squealed, and pulled it from his grasp.

He said something in troll, and everyone laughed. Kialessa looked around but the shamaness was nowhere to be seen. She was secretly disappointed; the shamaness was like good luck.

'Pretty little human, they tell me you're part tree, but I don't see the resemblance.' Trolls laughed.

'Appearances can be… deceiving,' Allastassia said, glancing at Kia.

'Oh, no one knows that better than me! You want to know where I got the *greenflame sabre*? A little **dog** gave it to me!' and he roared with laughter.

The trolls joined in, except for the troll general who was always by his side. Kialessa noted a concerned look on the general's face, as though his warlord had just said something he really should not have.

And Kialessa realised she had some very important

information the next time she saw her king.

Suddenly the warlord hit Allastassia. It didn't look like he intended it to be a very hard hit, but he was inhumanly strong. Allastassia was flung to the ground, hard.

Amusingly, the trolls seemed more shocked than entertained.

Before she could barely rise, the troll warlord grabbed her by the throat and lifted her into the air. 'Now, pale enchantress. You will die for me so that we can finally get this war started!' he threw her away, yet with a dancer's grace she twisted in the air and landed on her feet.

Kialessa watched the warlord turn his back on Allastassia. She saw him reaching for a knife at his belt, and with a stabbing pain Kialessa realised her friend had only moments to live.

Allastassia put that time to good use. Her hair and dress twisted around in an invisible breeze as she commanded the magic. With a twinkle in her eye a wave of energy spread around her, and Kialessa's hair stood on end as the static electricity washed passed her.

The warlord paused, and turned to glare at her.

Allastassia lifted herself up in a classical dance pose, and then crouched down and stomped her foot against the earth in the same way the trolls often did. In that very instant every drum in the entire arena thundered a single, powerful beat.

Allastassia opened her hand, palm down, in a dramatic fashion. The deep throated chorus of men trolls seemed to shake the ground. Kialessa watched over, some of them seem surprised they were singing, others watched Allastassia with devoted attention. It seemed Allastassia was putting her powers of commanding others attention to some very good use.

Again, the drums sounded, taking up a rapid, rhythmic beat.

And Allastassia danced.

Moving like fire, trailing lightning, Allastassia picked up the song in a frantic, thunderous rhythm. Troll young and old soon picked up the beat. She looked fabulous, and utterly unafraid.

But she danced as though her life depended on it.

The song she wove through her enchantments was captivating. It was a genius weave of Lenmer'el songs and troll percussion – it was likely she'd been preparing it all day. Thunder and music swelled in a passionate, thrilling dance. Trolls seemed almost unable to help themselves from joining in.

All the while Ki-Taieri watched with dark admiration.

Suddenly Kialessa felt a shift in the music; the air seemed to start pulsing with a new rhythm. From the edge of the arena some trolls were approaching, and they brought with them a powerful counterpoint to Allastassia's improvised melody. A chorus of over a hundred trolls was approaching. They wore wooden armour, and banged sticks against their own chests to augment the thrumming of their powerful footfalls. And they sang a consonant resonance of soul refining power. Kialessa felt the hair on her neck stick up, and her arms prickled with the thrill of their music. A hundred troll musicians, each with as much command of magic and sound as Allastassia had. Command, and appreciation. They clearly loved what Allastassia had brought to their party.

Soon they began to drown her out, and for a moment Allastassia faltered. She watched them with burning eyes and fevered breath. She set her jaw and grinned - it was clear she was not going to let them take her stage.

The battle was joined, the two songs merged and fought. Two troll minstrels, nostrils flaring and trumpets blaring raced to the front. They confronted Allastassia with a fevered dance and raw melody of their own making. Allastassia responded, causing her musicians to imitate and improve their sound, adding blinding bass and an unparalleled countermelody. The minstrels laughed, and quickly retreated.

The music turned dark, and in walked a troll man, covered in runic markings and what looked like scriptures written on flowing parchments; a liturgist. He invoked some kind of ancient troll melody from the ground itself that Kialessa had never heard before. It made the trolls gasp, and some wept. Kialessa had no idea what the song meant, but it was clearly very important to the trolls.

Allastassia's music died. For a moment there was silence. Then, possessed by sound alone, the two troll

     By Dr Joe Ireland

trumpeters stood by *her* side. They lifted their polished bronze instruments to their lips, and played a single, solemn duet back. The sound penetrated the silence and echoed in the darkness further than she could imagine. Kialessa knew that song. It was the anthem of Emerel. A sacred tune of their own that spoke of the eternal debt each life owed their own country. A tune that begged from all no sacrifice too great for the love of their people, not even their own lives.

The trolls did not know the tune, but they understood it.

The liturgist nodded, and without moving invoked a song in counterpoint to her own. Then Kialessa realised it was the troll hymn.

Unbidden tears rose to her eyes and Kialessa felt the anthems of the two mighty nations were, indeed, a perfect companion to the other. They seemed to sanctify and exalt, support and yet celebrate the other. Troll voices soon joined a chorus, the ground itself beating a thunderous bass and rhythm. The anthems swelled in the night, till they harmonised to a perfect, thunderous conclusion.

Troll voices roared their applause, yet despite the sound Kialessa was suddenly drawn to a new sound. It came from across the hill, from across the Broadwaters. She wasn't sure how she could hear it, yet it was clear to her ears… the soldiers of Lenmer'el were applauding the performance as well.

A silhouette caught her attention, and there she saw

her, the old troll shamaness. She was staring right at Kialessa, and sniffed her amused derision out towards the Broadwaters.

Kialessa couldn't help but smile at the old troll.

But there was still a very real problem to attend to.

Soon the applause began to die down, and everyone turned to look at the troll warlord.

He smiled, and looked touched. He shrugged, and his people laughed. Then he shouted something at Allastassia in troll.

'What!' she demanded to know.

'He says there is no point killing you now,' the shamaness shouted above the rabble, 'since next season he will make of you another wife!'

Trolls cheered.

Allastassia screamed even louder this time, 'WHAT!'

The trolls laughed, and Ki-Taieri gave her a mocking bow.

Instantly Allastassia advanced on the warlord, lightning forming into a javelin in her hand. The troll elite were there in a blink, draw weapons blocking her path.

Few of the trolls were laughing now.

Ki-Taieri said something again, something foolish and light-hearted while hidden behind a forest of a hundred spears, wielded by his fanatical followers ready to die for him in an instant.

Allastassia screamed, raising her weapon. But the warlord didn't look in the least phased. The shamaness

     By Dr Joe Ireland

raised her fist, and ripping the javelin out of Allastassia's hand discharged it into the ground.

With a huff, Allastassia stormed back to the prison and completely paralysed a guard who tried to stand in her way. Then she pulled open the prison door, walked in, and with both hands and a squeal of defiance, slammed herself in.

The warlord waved dismissively, said something unkind that made the trolls laugh again, and turned his back on them all to continue his drinking. He told the musicians to start up again, but their music had lost its magic now. It was simply … rhythm again, though it got the trolls dancing.

The liturgist looked like he was going to speak to Allastassia, but the shamaness stood in his way. There was a brief conversation, but she put her hand on his chest. He grunted, nodded once at Allastassia, and walked away.

Kialessa turned to look at Allastassia. She was curled up in a ball in the back of the prison, Darrix sitting beside her.

No one bothered to lock the prison door. Silently, Kialessa opened it, and walked in to check on her friends.

Glass coloured tears rimmed the enchantress's large eyes, and her lip quivered. But she said nothing.

Kialessa said nothing, but she let her arms slip around Allastassia, and hugged her tight.

Suddenly Darrix stood.

The shamaness was at their prison door. She looked

like she was about to say something, when Darrix replied, 'I know.'

She huffed. 'For all, I have prayed. For the other four, I could see a way out, a chance, if they thanked their stars and behaved themselves wisely.'

Darrix nodded.

'Stop doing that, it means you give honour. If you agree, grunt, from here,' she said, slapping her stomach.

Darrix agreed.

She agreed back at him. Then she sighed, 'For all… but you. Full blooded human; and a male with little to offer but the threat of becoming a man. You are tall; we don't like that among our kind, for becoming tall makes fools of us. Your height offends us, for we are jealous. And then you cover yourselves with metal, and polish it as if the earth offends you! And then you stare, oh, how you stare! The burning eyes of men, always watching, always judging and sneering. We make an elixir of your eyes to make us fierce. The price of a manslave with two eyes is high in these parts.'

Allastassia clutched her fists.

The old shamaness looked in sadly. 'But I see no safety for you, manling. The warlord needs only your pelt … I fear … there is nothing I can do for you here.'

'Then why do anything for us at all?' Darrix asked.

She sighed, resting to within easy reach of all within the prison. Her voice… seemed tired. 'I do not want a war, manling. Green blood should not flow on such un-sacred

     By Dr Joe Ireland

lands, and for such an unworthy cause. My people do not want a war.'

'They seem very eager to me,' Allastassia accused the old lady.

She grunted, 'Some are. But the rest? We are not warriors. Despite what your hate filled eyes have been trained to see, young enchantress, we are not all keen to battle for glory. We are musicians, and scholars. We are hunters, and gatherers. We live in harmony with the land, and we want to watch our children grow old by the light of our own hearth fire.' Her voice broke, as though reminded of a memory still painful.

Kialessa looked up at her. 'What happened?' she asked the old woman.

She glanced at her, tears in her eyes. 'What good will such knowledge give you?' she demanded, and put her back to them all.

'Please,' Allastassia begged, kneeling, and seemed to want to put the touch of magic into those words.

The old shamaness grunted; she was not deceived by the enchantress's guile. But she spoke anyway, 'He was Ra Puanga, the beloved of my youth. We would chase each other by the mānga-a-huripapa, until I let him catch me. We talked of our children and of our lives together. It was such an honour to be courted by the son of great chief! How his father hated out mating, but I was too gifted to ignore. Our wedding, such an honour! The flame flowers, the red and yellow! The party did not die down for three whole days!' she sighed.

No one interrupted. They let her speak.

'But then there was Ki-Taieri. Four years ago he arrives in our kingdom, the exiled son of a forgotten prince. He claims the throne, and calls our people to the ritual trial of chiefs. By what arts unknown to me, though I suspect it was poison… he bested my Ra in single combat. He claimed the kingdom, and with it, my hand in marriage.'

Kialessa didn't know what to say.

Allastassia gasped. 'And now he claims your people for the war.'

'Not mine alone, no. All the five kingdoms must come to his war. But without the spear he fears he cannot claim their faithful devotion – and he is right. Yet none have found the worth in their soul to claim the great warlord's spear, though many have died trying in the past three hundred years.'

'And now he feels driving the Great Kingdom to war will help him achieve that?' Darrix asked.

She huffed, 'Ki-Taieri cares not for the lives of his people, even less than the lives of the other troll nations. No, he craves not wealth, or land, or women. His lust is but one – infamy. He wants to be *feared*.'

'Well, I'm terrified,' Allastassia admitted.

The shamaness grunted in sympathy, then looked gravely at Darrix. 'So, don't die tomorrow, if you can help it. All right?'

Darrix grunted.

     By Dr Joe Ireland

# The Sacrifice

*'If I die, then at least I die knowing all of you, my four closest friends, are beside me, and you are all free.'*

*Darrix, the prayerful warrior. From 'The year in jail', chapter, 'Stupid things Darrix has said.'*

Kialessa woke with a start. The dawn was quite bright, and she was used to waking up much earlier. She looked around in alarm to make sure everyone was there.

Darrix was kneeling in his armour, praying. Allastassia had taken all the provender she could from the beasts to make herself a bed, and looked to be so asleep nothing but the imposition of magic might awaken her. Piex and Posk were still nowhere to be seen.

And Eclipse had fled.

Kialessa went to the door of the unlocked prison to see if something had awoken her.

There was shouting from the warlord's tent. She smiled to herself, wondering if someone else was regretting sleeping in.

He burst out and continued shouting. Soldiers were up in an instant. The entire area was still a mess from last night's party, but it was cleaned up with almost supernatural haste once the trolls saw the kind of mood their warlord was in.

It did not bode well for Darrix.

The warlord sat, steaming, on his throne.

Without waiting to be asked Darrix strode out towards the arena. He was fully armed and, Kialessa noted, as polished as he could be under the circumstances. He stood up tall.

The trolls responded instantly, spitting at his feet and mocking him. A few even reached out, and slapped him.

Darrix bore it all without a complaint or retribution.

Kialessa and Allastassia ran down to the arena. No one impeded them till they were at its edge, then the elite guard made sure they went no further with drawn spears and spiked clubs. A moment later Allastassia pointed, Piex and Posk had joined them. They both looked like they'd gotten a very good night's sleep, and both appeared to be wearing some kind of troll … study robes. Posk was even carrying a scroll.

 By Dr Joe Ireland

Posk dropped his bundle and rushed toward Darrix, blocking his way. 'You watch your shield arm, shiny,' his looked worried. 'They like to catch it and throw you with it still on. All right? And don't, slice. Stab. Take them out; don't try to wear us down. All right? You'll be all right?' his voice broke and he looked away.

'Don't worry about me,' Darrix said after a moment, resting his hand on the younger boy's shoulder. 'Our king will not cross into these lands to claim my skin; tell him he must not. I will find my peace regardless of how I die or where I am buried, or even if I am never buried. Don't worry about me. If I die, then at least I die knowing all of you, my four closest friends, are beside me, and you are all free.'

And with that Darrix walked into the centre of the arena, alone.

Suddenly the warlord roared. The entire hoard fell swiftly silent.

'Beg,' the warlord ordered.

For a moment, Darrix just stood there. Then he began to draw his legendary sword, Defender.

The trolls jeered and mocked.

Darrix waited till they fell silent. He finished drawing his sword, and with one smooth motion, threw it at the feet of the warlord. Impressively, it landed point down in the soil.

Darrix looked at the warlord's feet, and looked meek even as he sounded courageous. 'The people of the Great

Kingdom do not seek war with the trolls of the far wilderness!'

The trolls mocked, and spat at him.

Darrix waited till they were quiet again. When he spoke, it was not a shout, and the trolls had to strain to hear him. 'No one win this war, mighty king. It will be the end of both our peoples-'

'Lies!' the general roared. 'He doubts the strength of trolls!'

Again, they mocked him, throwing fetid vegetables at him.

That was when Kialessa realised that no one was mocking her. Or shoving her. She looked around, and realised with a start that all the trolls guarding her and Allastassia were marked with the same totems as the shamaness.

'Allastassia, look!' Kialessa whispered, 'the trolls here are protecting us.'

Allastassia looked bemused, but as she looked about the same realisation finally dawned on her as well. The trolls that had been guarding their prison were protecting it as well.

But no such protections were provided Darrix right now. He stood out there in the open, in the armour that they all hated, and without a weapon in his reach. But she'd seen him face down similar odds with just as much courage. She just knew he'd find a way out of this one too. He just had to…

　　　　　　By Dr Joe Ireland

When they fell silent enough to hear him, Darrix explained. 'None can contest the trolls for strength, or number.' They agreed. 'All within the kingdom live in fear of the day the trolls return!' here they cheered him on. Now Darrix shouted, 'None can speak the name of TotoMuru without knowing *fear*!'

They roared their approval, but still threw things at him. Then they let him speak again.

Softly, he continued, 'Yet… none within that kingdom have lived to see what I have seen of the trolls.' They sneered. 'I have seen kindness I never knew existed in your people. I have watched you… help each other, and sing… you nurture the earth in ways my people have never considered! You have scholars, the wit and wisdom of the greatest in the whole Great Kingdom! You have musicians who know songs that have almost torn my soul in half.'

They did not argue.

'Why, mighty king? When my people still have so much to learn from you? Teach us… teach me,' and he bowed to his knee. 'I give myself your servant for life. My life, for my peoples.'

Kialessa felt her heart prick. Allastassia gasped loud enough for everyone to hear. A slave for life? They would make elixir out of one of his eyes, and a potion from his blood every day he lived among them… for the rest of his life.

The warlord actually seemed to be considering it.

Kialessa looked around; it now looked like the four other kings were there now, saying nothing. But they did not look at Ki-Taieri.

The liturgist and was there, and the beast hunter, and the chief scholar. All said nothing.

With a roar the warlord stood. 'Never!' He continued shouting in troll, his war band trying to work everyone into a frenzy. But no one participated with any enthusiasm. Then he seemed to say something that the other trolls did not like. The four kings stood, and started shouting at him. Trolls began shoving and yelling at each other all over the arena.

But all fell to unadulterated silence when Ki-Taieri drew out the greenflame sabre.

Piex moved over so he could translate, "You see, the human defiles even us with his **poison** words. This is their way, to make a friend of one while we turn on each other, and to wipe us all out in the end! Death, death to the humans!"

His powerful chanting drew a swift crowd, who soon drowned out any dissenting voices. He made a swift gesture towards the beast master, who did not move. The warlord made the gesture again, more forcefully this time, and the beast master left.

Trolls were still shouting when the monster arrived.

The earth suddenly shuddered, and seemed to turn into black soil under her feet. The sky turned red as a noise split the air, a devastating howl unlike anything she had

     By Dr Joe Ireland

ever heard before. Again the earth thundered, and entire troll hoard parted as something massive approached. It was a moving hill in the shape of a stone bore, or wolf, it was impossible to tell. Its eyes, covered with rune engraved leather, glowed with red fire. Its breath was fire, and its fur was like great rods of iron. And as it stood, the ground seemed to give way under its feet.

Piex was pale. 'It is the Atua-haka, the divine beast. The living spirit of war.'

It seemed to sense its moment had arrived. The two largest trolls of the entire army struggled with all their might using titanium collars on broad poles to steer the beast in the direction of the arena. Trolls leapt out of its way, but two weren't fast enough. It gorged one to pieces, and ate the other one whole.

Darrix turned, and glanced at them.

Kialessa would have run in there to help him, but strong troll arms held her back.

Suddenly the arena filled with steam as the demidemon breathed at them. Wildfire leapt up from its back, and it dug its feet into the ground. Thunder rumbled in the distant sky, and black clouds gathered in moments.

Yet a thin light pierced the darkness from the direction of the horizon. Kialessa turned to see the clouds had not crossed the Broadwaters, turning silver the edges of the dark nimbus. But the trolls ignored that, roaring in hatred at everything human. Their faces grew dark in the suddenly fading light.

Allastassia screamed out at Darrix, but he simply waited.

The ground shook. It seemed the entire Great Kingdom was looking at them all right now. A million souls, and even more, begging Darrix to win this fight and save them all.

But Darrix just stood there, not even reaching for his sword.

The trolls were standing well back by now, the arena edge bristling with every spear available. Kialessa was almost crushed by the throng, till she climbed up a troll to stand on his hips and hold on to his neck. He either didn't mind, or didn't notice.

Somehow the ground in the arena began to sink down into a gentle depression, Darrix at the centre.

With a roar from the warlord, they removed the blinding helm over the monster's eyes, and it fixed a burning gaze at Darrix. An instant later, it charged, burning coals leaping up from the ground in its gait, the air turning to steam as it ran.

Darrix did not budge, but with one knee on the ground simply knelt there.

Steam and thunder bore down on Darrix as the ambassador of death, yet he did not move.

Kialessa expected him to leap aside at the last instant, but that instant came, and went.

And the Atua-haka stopped dead in its tracks, its head almost touching Darrix. Steam and coals wrapped around the young man, and for a moment he was lost from her sight. But as the air cleared, Darrix still knelt there, unharmed, unmoving, eyes closed as though praying.

The trolls cheered, and the Atua-haka roared. There was no sound like it to Kialessa's ears. It tore at her spirit and almost killed her where she stood. The strength left her, and her fingers slipped from the troll she was standing on. But he and the others roared, seeming to gain strength and courage from that sonic attack, and she held tight once more.

But Darrix did not move.

The divine beast strode around him, fixing him with its gaze. The ground trembled as it passed, the scent of deep forests passing over her almost forcing her mind into a trance. She wondered how Darrix could simply… kneel there.

Again the beast roared, and Darrix waited, unmoving. It seemed the beast was unwilling to attack anyone who did not flee, or fight for their life.

Then he moved, and the beast charged. But it stopped dead when he paused, and watched with puzzlement as he removed his helm and put it on the ground next to him.

'Patua ia, patua ia!' the warlord roared repeatedly.

The trolls were edging the beast on, but it ignored them. Its gaze was fixed only on Darrix.

Then Darrix raised his hand, palm out.

The Atua-haka looked at it, and roared in disbelief.

'He seeks to tame it?' Allastassia shouted with equal

incredulity.

The beast roared again, the flames on its back reaching high into the air, dark smoke streaming upwards to join the darkened clouds in the sky. Again and again it charged against Darrix, but it seemed unable to bring itself to harm him while he refused to flee, or to defend himself. Again and again, while the troll warlord grew angrier and angrier. Every time it charged in, it pulled back, yet each time the distance it fled was less than previously. It grew closer, and closer.

Suddenly the deadly flames disappeared, and the trembling in the ground fell silent. With an almost gentle movement the Atua-haka sniffed at Darrix's outstretched hand.

The trolls fell silent. Time seemed to pause around them again as every troll held their breath.

Then the impossible happened, as the mighty elemental demidemon pressed its forehead gently to the palm of the paladin squire's outstretched hand. The entire ground gave a tremulous shaking as though something of enormous power had passed between them.

'Ehe!' the warlord shouted.

Without a pause Darrix stood up, and as the beast knelt down, he climbed up on its foot, pulled himself up to its knee, and then again up onto its neck. It thundered with agreement.

The warlord roared again, and trolls began to move around. Atua-haka looked around in threat, but Darrix stilled him. Without a fight, they allowed the trolls to drag Darrix from the beast even as they clamped the collars on it once more. Atua-haka fought, throwing all away from him, cutting up the troll elite that tried to tie him down.

Kialessa turned, and watched the troll shamaness do nothing but watch.

Fire erupted from the beast again, and it turned to its new rider.

'Go!' Darrix ordered.

Atua-haka roared.

'Go!' Darrix repeated.

With a baleful cry, an impressive whirlwind struck up around the beast. Dirt and earth were thrown everywhere, and a moment later the mighty Atua-haka was gone, a titanium collar lying sundered on the ground.

Trolls were shouting. The four kings looked livid, their guards pressing against the warlord's remaining elite. He suffered their shouting for a good three moments.

Then, drawing the greenflame sabre he stabbed it into the earth. The trolls fell silent as fire leapt out and circled the hill at the end of the arena.

The warlord looked at them grimly, and Piex translated his words, "So, you want your enemies to tell me how to run our kingdom? Who I can marry, or who I cannot kill? You are all fools. Bring all the children of our enemies to the hill of trial *right now*. I challenge them all to the sacred right of rulership. I am going to kill them in front of your eyes. Then we will see who rules beyond the

Broadwaters, and who does not!"

 By Dr Joe Ireland

# The Hill Of Trial

*Vulnerability is the father of belonging.*
*Eclipse, 318CY*

There was nowhere to go.

Kia watched with surreal dread as the trolls hauled all five of them off to the hill. The green flames parted in their steps.

They only had a moment to chat; it felt so much like preparing for battle at the college that it was, for a moment, so familiar.

'We're all going to die,' Piex mourned.

7 Drunk, angry, and careless, the troll king would still prove a formidable foe

 By Dr Joe Ireland

'We've got this,' Allastassia interrupted. 'He's drunk, he's angry. It's going to be easy to get him to make a mistake.'

'He's strong,' Posk added.

'How do we take this guy down?' Kialessa wondered out loud.

'Don't match his strength with your own, no matter what,' Darrix told him. 'Keep out of his way. Don't let him touch you.'

Posk agreed. He had his gauntlets on, and he ripped the scholar robes off in the next moment.

'I leant a new troll spell,' Piex said. 'It gives bones the strength of stone, for a moment. But they cannot heal for a while.'

'That's not much help,' Allastassia complained. 'He'll break all our bones, stone or not.'

Everyone agreed.

Piex looked sad. 'At least there's this. Kialessa, hand me your whip,' he muttered arcane words as he wrote something with a golden stylus on the back of the hilt. 'I've been meaning to do this for weeks, but we only got the ingredients from the troll sages last night. I taught them how to do it. It's a rune that will make an object fire resistant, for a short time. You can use your wizardry on the whip now,' he said, handing it back. 'This rune will protect it. You can set your whip on fire, and it will not burn.'

Kialessa was impressed, this was a great advantage. A

few weeks late, perhaps. But a flaming weapon was still an impressive weapon.

'Just use the term *instrumentum in manibus* rather than *ignis didgitis* to enact the spell, understood.'

She nodded. At least it was something. And her father would be so very impressed when she showed him what his old whip could do when she got home at winter's dawn.

If she ever saw him again.

They looked over at the warlord, his general wrapping up his hands for battle. He was a seasoned, skilled, and famous warrior – a king. Kialessa had to admit that it did not look hopeful her and her friends. There were no drums to save them, no scholars to plead for them.

At best, all that waited for them was noble death.

Trolls approached them, bearing Darrix's sword and Kialessa's whip. They offered them some kind of brew, probably to still death's pain. But they all refused it. They stood in a circle so that Darrix could offer his customary prayer before battle when the shamaness approached.

She looked broken, and terribly sorry. She looked at them each in turn, and didn't speak. Then, drawing up clay from the ground, anointed their cheeks. Kialessa felt the fire of her blessing flow through her, every weariness of the past week fleeing at her touch. She bowed with gratitude.

'I wish you could have stayed a little longer,' she muttered.

Posk barked angrily. 'The troll king executes us for no crime, so that he can start a war he does not deserve? Pah, I do not belong here.'

She grunted.

In emphasis Posk tore at the tattoo they'd given him, looking like he might rip his own skin off to be rid of the stain of unjust king. He looked confused when it didn't just wipe off. Allastassia had to hold his arms down.

Darrix stood up, 'Here, like this,' and with a prayer of faith wiped his hand down Posk's arm. The ink fled out instantly, smearing down his arm. The tattoo then brushed away without scar as Posk rubbed the dirt against it.

The shamaness pressed back her tears at the sight. 'Give him a fight to remember, children,' she begged them. 'Give him cause to respect the shining shields, burning magic, and fierce eyes of men.'

Posk agreed, and held her arm. He looked in her eyes, and showed he was unafraid.

She sobbed, and held his arm. It seemed she could say no more, and left.

Darrix spoke, 'At least, let us leave a scar. Something to be remembered by. Aim for his face.'

'Forget that,' Allastassia demanded. 'We're taking this guy down and having dinner this season in our king's hall. *Got it!*'

They all had to agree, but only Posk seemed to believe her.

Drums thundered from the hundreds of trolls

gathered behind the green flames. It was time.

The mighty warlord Ki-Taieri began to circle them warily, though he still looked as though he had not yet recovered from last night's party. 'You've cost me a great deal of time, humans. But you now pay for it with your lives. Be thankful that you will not live to see your houses torn down and your cities burn.'

8 The five battle Ki-Taieri

They answered nothing, but kept in a tight battle pose. Posk knelt at front, gauntlets raised in defence. Darrix took

　　　　By Dr Joe Ireland

the left, his shield protecting them all. Kialessa took the right, burning whip tense in her hand. Piex stood in the centre, barely tall enough to look over Posk, and Allastassia held the rear, levitating herself up into the air her shield of ice spell already defending them from attacks from behind.

'What, no witty words of defiance? No stealing our music or our beasts?'

'You die today,' Posk informed him.

Ki-Taieri laughed, 'No, you do.' And with that he threw the sabre at them.

It flew so fast – it was barely visible in its motion. Posk moved as though he hoped to lose an arm to protect them, but one other motion caught Kialessa's eye, a gentle rising up of some spirit from the soil. Two great horns, like antlers, appeared from the earth. A great, dark, disc of energy that rested between the horns met the flying sabre head on, and with a dreadful clang that rocked her bones and filled the air with green and black sparks, the disc deflected the sabre far away to the other end of the battlefield.

For an instant Eclipse, the dragon, stood there. She was entirely see-through, a non-corporeal. 'One day I must remember to thank my father,' she whispered to Kialessa.

'Now!' Allastassia shouted, quick to catch on.

Blinding lightning fell from the sky, momentarily stunning the warlord. He bore it with little effort, but it gave them the chance they desperately needed to charge.

Posk drove into him with a flurry of desperate blows that made the warlord stagger backwards. But the seasoned warrior recovered quickly, and grabbing Posk's face threw him several paces away without effort. Darrix was there, and swinging Defender almost hit the warlord in his head, who ducked at the very last instant. Bringing up his fist he almost struck Darrix in his chest, but the young man stepped lively away. Golden shackles reached up from the ground, trapping the warlord momentarily. Darrix swung again, but Ki-Taieri used the chains to protect himself from the blow. He wrapped the chain around the sword and almost pulled it away, but Darrix was expecting the move. With straining power Ki-Taieri ripped the chains in pieces, something that no human had ever before achieved. He swung a severed chain at Darrix, who stepped right and protected them all with his shield. The warlord drew back as if to use the chain to grab the shield, but Darrix jabbed forward and, though the warlord moved too fast to land a telling blow, cut the troll along his collar.

A hail of lightning stuck the warlord in his chest, for a moment blinding them all. Allastassia had never wielded so much lightning at once, but the troll just laughed.

Posk returned, flanking with Darrix, and they both charged. Swinging around with gauntlet and sword the two young men tried to find an opening in the warlord's defences, but it was to little avail. The warlord was just toying with them, dodging, blocking with his arms,

     By Dr Joe Ireland

striking out with such ferocity they had to pull back. He absorbed more lightning, and Allastassia looked drained, but Ki-Taieri just laughed again. Kialessa held back, looking for her opening, hoping to catch his ankle, or eye… some way to give the advantage to her allies.

Dark daggers of light flew from the mist at the warlord, probably Eclipse's contribution, but he defected them all. A *magus sphere* appeared, and he caught it in his bare hand, crushing it as it exploded. It would have hurt terribly, but he just laughed again.

Somehow, in the distraction, Posk landed a solid blow to his left ribs. Now the warlord looked annoyed. He caught Darrix's sword in his wrapped right hand, and might have snapped it but Darrix guessed the move and went with it.

Then Ki-Taieri stomped on the ground. The rippling wave of energy was so much more than shifting earth. Kialessa felt all her bones jar at the force, and for a moment she could barely move.

Curiously, Ki-Taieri did not take his advantage to kill any of them just yet. Instead, he leapt far way, almost to the other edge of the battlefield.

Right to within a few paces of his greenflame sabre.

'Gather!' Allastassia yelled, no doubt hoping to put themselves behind Eclipse's unbreakable shield.

So, naturally, Kialessa ran in the opposite direction – *toward* the troll king. Just as he was reaching down to pick his sword up from the earth, she lashed out her whip and grabbed it by the hilt. With a tug she pulled it to the ground. Instead of lunging for it, the warlord looked over at her. With a squeal she didn't really mean to make, Kialessa hauled the sword out of his reach and toward her friends.

They took their cue and ran toward it, but Kialessa was still closer. She leapt and reached out her hand.

Quickly she realised it was a terrible mistake. The sword burst into scorching green fire. The message was clear – it would not let her touch it.

Ki-Taieri laughed once more.

The others arrived. Darrix prayed fervently, but knew his god did not grant him the power to wield the weapon. Eclipse went to sunder it, but pulled back as it burst into flames. Allastassia picked it up with electricity, but it slipped from her grasp. Piex… seemed to stand there, probably trying to read the troll runes along its side.

'Get it, don't let him touch it!' Allastassia shouted.

'That's not going to work,' Eclipse droned.

'Can we find a way to neutralise its efficacy, even temporarily?' Piex offered.

'I don't understand why my prayer didn't help,' Darrix wondered.

'Just get it out of the circle!' Kialessa demanded.

Posk didn't say anything. Kialessa took just a moment to register that at some point he'd lost his only other tusk in the fight, blood trailing down his lip, but he just battled on.



By Dr Joe Ireland

There was a thump, and they all turned to see Ki-Taieri leaping through the air at them. They jumped back, fully expecting another bone jarring earth-thump when he landed. But Posk leapt forward.

Gripping the sword hilt in both hands, oblivious to the green flames as his eyes turned black with rage, he swept up the sword so quickly none could have avoided it. Ki-Taieri reared back as he hit the ground, losing his chance to thump the earth, but narrowly managing to avoid getting skewered as well. He stood there, looking at Posk, his face a mix of curiosity and surprise.

Green fire flowed all around Posk, and he roared. The earth stood up around his ankles, covering his feet. Green fire roared up, covering him, protecting him. And as Kialessa watched, the sword's fire glowed green in his eyes.

'Ahu!' roared Ki-Taieri.

Posk swung wide. The sword seemed heavy in his grasp. Ki-Taieri stepped back. Darrix lunged, trying to get around to his back, and Allastassia drove near, her hands covered in lightning. Again, and again Posk swung the sabre, seeming to become stronger and more skilled at every stroke. The warlord was forced back, barley keeping the two swords at bay with his bare hands, now cut and bleeding. They kept the pressure up.

9 Kialessa and Eclipse battle the troll king

The warlord stomped again, but they were ready this time. Even so, it was just enough of a distraction for the Ki-Taieri to lunge forward, and grip the hilt of his sabre in Posk's hands. They wrestled for a moment, Darrix stabbing the warlord right in the side and he didn't even seem to notice. Ki-Taieri pulled at the sabre, and Posk was no match for his strength. It flung away in the air, and Ki-Taieri turned and leapt after it.

Posk was fast, and punching his gauntleted fists into the ground, roared. The ground near the sabre split into a deep crevice, and the weapon tiled towards it. Allastassia

     By Dr Joe Ireland

whispered some arcane word, and a gentle breeze raced past them and pushed the sword into the crack. Posk released his hold on the earth, and it snapped shut even as Ki-Taieri punched it, hard. He tried to dig down, pulling at the earth with superhuman strength, but could not reach it in time. In a punitive gesture the warlord flung dirt at them.

It stung like bees, thrown with incredible furry. Ki-Taieri charged them this time, attacking with unbridled power. He flung Posk aside, and threw him at Piex. Eclipse slithered around, but was struck too hard in her side that she fell over painfully. Then he roared at Allastassia and the lightning that she held, a primitive growl of such power she stumbled backwards. He didn't seem to notice Kialessa was there. Darrix was on him, and before anyone could recover Ki-Taieri ducked his sword and stuck Darrix in the leg with his outstretched hand. They could hear the bone in Darrix's leg breaking from where they stood.

Darrix knelt, and Ki-Taieri said nothing, nor did he move to finish him. But the old troll breathed heavily, 'Well done, kids. You do your people proud. But now, you die.' Then in an inexplicable tactical error, he walked away to try and dig up his sabre again.

They gathered around Darrix. He prayed, and the bleeding stopped but the bone did not knit back together. Kialessa tried to help, but neither Piex's nor Eclipse's great knowledge could assist. Allastassia reached down into the earth, rapidly growing up wooden vines and trying to encase Darrix's leg in a splint.

Then Posk, still burning with black fire rage, grabbed the leg and roared at it.

The bone snapped back into place, whole and mended.

'Oh, all right then,' Darrix expressed their mutual surprise.

'We need a plan,' Allastassia was breathing heavily.

No one spoke.

'I can turn his bones into stone?' Piex muttered.

Posk grunted his agreement.

It only took Darrix a moment to realise what Posk already knew. 'Stone! Inanimate! Those gauntlets will do extra damage to inanimate objects, you remember?'

'I believe your conjecture is accurate!' Piex said, getting excited.

'What?' Eclipse hummed.

'If we are able to make his bones into stone, even for a moment, we might have an unforeseen advantage,' Piex explained.

'Greater compressive strength, less flexibility...?' Eclipse was trying to figure it out.

'The gauntlets!' Allastassia pointed at Posk's fists.

'Oh!' Eclipse finally understood.

'He's going to get that sabre,' Kialessa noted.

'Not through me,' Eclipse informed them, and turning into a ghost dragon once more disappeared into the earth.

'Wait for the right moment, spread out,' Allastassia

　　　　By Dr Joe Ireland

told them.

They advanced on the warlord, Kialessa and Piex trying to hide in the shadows on either side.

'Hey, warlord!' Darrix shouted, standing up uninjured.

Ki-Taieri glanced over, and looked angry. Then he kept digging, looking quite frustrated.

'Whomever said you were an unfit leader was totally wrong,' Allastassia teased him. 'See? You do us the kind favour of digging your own grave today.'

He glared at her, and returned to his project, looking now confused. He had probably met with Eclipse's interference.

'The earth… is not his friend,' even Posk teased him, though words seemed difficult right now. 'She hides his treasures … from unworthy hands.'

That upset him. He roared, and dug. Then, with a grimace and a grin, he tore a ghost dragon out of the ground and flung her through the air.

They tried to charge, but green fire burst from the hole and held them momentarily back as he reached in and grabbed the sabre.

Roaring like thunder Posk leapt high into the air. Ki-Taieri gripped his blade and with perfect certainly Kia knew it would be Posk's doom.

But to get a better aim, he took a step backwards.

Kialessa saw her first true chance today, and lashing out with her whip grabbed his ankle just before it touched the ground. She had no hope of stopping it, but could put it out of alignment, and the drunk troll began to stumble. He lowered the sword and looked down to get his footing.

Lightning flashed down from a darkened sky, blinding him. Piex uttered words of arcane power, words she knew would turn a creature's bones temporarily to stone. And stone, he had pointed out, was far more inanimate than bone.

Darrix moved in with sword drawn. Kia knew he couldn't hope to do much damage now, but a well-placed jab might still take out an eye and of this, Ki-Taieri was completely aware. At the last instant Darrix lashed out, forcing the troll to shield his face.

And that was when Posk struck. Like the thunder crashing from the heavens, he flew from the sky to strike the troll lord squarely on the side of his face with all his engaged might, armoured with his magical gauntlets.

There was a sickening crunch that brought the entire hill to abject silence.

Ki-Taieri staggered under the blow, blood pouring from his mouth. His entire jaw hung limp, his eye bleeding, his face irreparably dented from Posk's single blow.

He whimpered, and staggered back again.

Posk moved to strike, but Darrix held him back for mercy's sake.

'Ahu …' Ki-Taieri muttered.

'You see! Free us, or die!' Darrix shouted. 'We –'



By Dr Joe Ireland

'NO!' Ki-Taieri roared. His men again found their rhythm, and beat their support to their wicked warlord. A sinister looked crossed his broken eye…

Ki-Taieri had reached the edge of the burning field, and turning to look out found what he was seeking. 'Hand me the spear,' he told his wife.

Her face burned with indignity. 'No! You finish the battle as the law demands – no new weapons in the arena!'

'Give it to me!' he roared.

She did not move.

'Give it to me, or you and your whole people die under my hand.'

She looked surprised, and afraid. Turning, she picked up the spear of TotoMuru.

'No!' Darrix roared. He tried to charge, but a motion from the warlord shook the earth and knocked them all down, yet the warlord almost fainted from the effort.

She placed the end of the spear through the green fire, and the warlord grabbed it.

Simultaneously many trolls outside the battle hill reached for their own faces as the spear's terrible power swept through them, taking their strength as his own.

Kia watched in dismay as the bone leapt back to its place, the blood receded, and colour returned to the punctured eye.

The trolls were in a riot. They roared in protest and fury, 'Dishonour, dishonour!'

His elite looked about with a mixture of concern and

fear.

Ki-Taieri ignored them all. 'It is but a little scratch,' he mocked them, yet in a voice so clear it was obvious his intoxicated state was ended as well. He ripped the spear out of his wife's hands, and held it high in the air with a roar of victory.

Kialessa's heart once again knew the gentle sorrow that acknowledged her life was about to end before its time. From this foe, there would be no retreat...

'Dishonour,' his wife whispered.

Ki-Taieri shook the spear, and laughed. 'Yes, yes! The spear of TotoMuru! The right to govern. It is mine, all is mine!' and his cruel laugher bit at the air.

So newly intoxicated was he with his great victory that he didn't even notice the white mist flowing up from around his feet. He didn't even feel the wet air gather around his knees.

He didn't see them until they were covered in mist. The drumming sounded further and further away. Within instants they were covered in shadow, the green fire almost invisible in the distance.

Ki-Taieri looked around, momentarily confused. Kialessa wondered where everyone but the warlord had gone; she could not even hear them in this thick mist.

Then the mist in front of the warlord began to gather together. In an instant it had formed a huge troll, the height of two regular trolls. He had black iron braces lined with thick wool, and his green skin was tattooed in red

                    By Dr Joe Ireland

blood. Within a heartbeat the spectre wrested the spear from Ki-Taieri's grip, and spun it in his hands like it belonged there.

He glared down at Ki-Taieri, unspeaking. The apparition's expression was one of supreme wisdom, and disappointment.

'To … TotoMuru…' Ki-Taieri uttered, his voice failing him in primal fear.

Then, without a word, the spirit of the great troll king drew itself up and stabbed Ki-Taieri in his chest.

Ki-Taieri crashed to the ground, and the spirit swiftly vanished.

The entire world seemed filled with an eerie silence. Kialessa called out, but only Darrix's voice was somewhat near.

She trembled as she walked towards the fallen form that was Ki-Taieri. He lay, scarcely breathing. His sword was just out the reach of his fingertips. He had tried to wield his sword, but not quick enough to stop the true troll warlord from smiting him into the soil. He looked up into the sky as though the heaven's judged him, commanding him to silence.

'Have you not found what you seek?' a troll woman's voice uttered, seeming to mock Kialessa.

She turned in fright, and saw his wife standing by his shoulder. Ki-Taieri acted as if he didn't know she was there.

'It was … it was…' Kialessa stuttered, lost for words.

Again, death had met her face to face. And yet, again, it had not claimed her. Relief, mingled with terrible fear that Ki-Taieri still breathed, struggled within her.

'I know,' the wife said. 'It was TotoMuru, true warlord of the peoples. He judged this man unworthy of his great blessing, and so he wrought upon himself his own punishment. Ki-Taieri is defeated.'

Kialessa looked down at the struggling troll, his breathing ragged. He didn't seem to have the strength of will to pull the spear from him, or the presence of mind to reach out to his unsheathed sword, only a hand's width away.

'What … what happens now?' Kialessa asked.

The shamaness was silent a moment, 'He is in your hands, child. Do what you feel you must.'

'He brought this on himself,' Kialessa realised.

His wife looked confused, 'You offer him pity? You turn him over to the judgements of his own people? The people he has corrupted, and offended even their own gods? You stay your hands even against this man who promised to slay you and all you ever loved!' She seemed angry, even incensed.

Kialessa could not watch the struggling troll. 'I do.'

The shamaness was silent a moment, hiding whatever inner turmoil troubled her. She did not seem impressed, or honoured at Kialessa's offer. Not in the least. 'Gah! Very well then. If so it must be. Come, child, bring me the spear.'

'Why don't you?' Kialessa asked.

          By Dr Joe Ireland

'Child!' the wife complained. 'Don't you see, I cannot enter this circle! Bring me the spear, then I will deliver Ki-Taieri to the justice he has earned. The spirit of TotoMuru has hallowed this place. We cannot enter until you bring the spear out.'

Kialessa took a step forward, finding her breath no easier than before. Never before had she been so close to death. She trembled as she walked up to the fallen warlord. His eyes were unfocused, his breathing shallow. He was clearly at the point of death.

For a moment her steps faltered. She briefly wondered if he was simply pretending. If this was just another test.

But then she remembered the terrifying vision of TotoMuru, and the fear fell from her heart. The true warlord had judged this pretender to the throne of the troll kings, and cast him down. And now they would deliver him to his people. And then, there would be no war.

With a steady resolve she reached out to grab the spear, knowing the legendary troll healing would keep him alive if this blow had not slain him.

Suddenly his wife held up her hand, and with a grasping gesture called down a bolt of blue lightning from the sky. It exploded into the butt of the spear, raced down the shaft through Kialessa's hand, and ran deep into Ki-Taieri's broken chest.

He died instantly.

Kialessa screamed, and tried desperately to pull the spear away. But she knew it was already too late. In that instant she realised her hand was firmly stuck to the spear. She tugged and tugged, trying to get her hand away. She didn't even notice how the fog had dissipated, or how the wife was now standing far away at the edge of the circle.

Or how a thousand trolls were now staring at her in horror and fear.

She didn't notice the wife's clutched hand, and her cunning smile. An instant later the troll raised her hand, and the spear leapt up from Ki-Taieri and into the air. Kialessa's hand still didn't let go, and she found herself standing with one foot on troll lord's chest, and with one hand she held the spear of TotoMuru high in the air.

Again silence fell.

'Kialessa,' Allastassia whispered.

'What,' Kialessa wondered.

'Scream.'

'Scream? Oh, scream,' drawing a huge breath, Kialessa let out a baleful wail that would be heard for by all. Its power surprised even her.

The trolls roared in horror, and exultation.

A moment later the elite charged them, but suddenly the ground underneath them split and rose high in the air. A voice was heard all across the savannah. Speaking in troll.

Kialessa didn't need to know what it said, because the troll elite began to throw their weapons to the ground. In the end most surrendered, though a few preferred to meet the judgement of their people.

     

Soon a chant was taken up, passing along from one troll to the next. The ground returned to its place, and great drums joined the new chorus.

Piex translated, "The tyrant king is dead."

10 Jindalessa; shamaness, warrior, queen

*Despite what your hate filled eyes have been trained to see, young enchantress, we are not all keen to battle for glory. We are musicians, and scholars. We are hunters, and gatherers. We live in harmony with the land, and we want to watch our children grow old by the light of our own hearth fire.*

*High Shamaness Jindalessa, cited by Allastassia, castle records CY 313*

'You WHAT?!' the steward roared at her.

Kialessa cringed, but did not look away. They were back in the king's pavilion, the six of them, not a moment to clean their boots. And they're brought with them five

 By Dr Joe Ireland

trolls.

The shamaness stood, seeming unimpressed, but Kialessa could not help but wonder if she saw with wiser eyes. The general was there, keen, alert, hand on the hilt of his wooden club imbedded with what might have been shark teeth. His eyes caught every movement, but he did not seem threatened. With them came the beast master and two of his surviving draygon, as well as the liturgist standing proudly, his ears shifting left and right to catch every noise. The newly appointed troll king, an elected leader of the council, the master of sages, led their expedition but did not speak.

'And that, Lord Grudon, was that,' the shamaness concluded. She had been telling him all about the defeat of Ki-Taieri, accurate in the retelling, right up to the part where Kialessa had held up the spear of the Blood Lord TotoMuru and not died. It left everyone with the impression that Kialessa had killed the warlord, lightning striking from the sky to seal the deed, rather than the more accurate retelling; it had all been Jindalessa once the foolish warlord had broken the oaths of battle. Kialessa wasn't comfortable with that version of the retelling, but held her peace. It had stopped a war, after all.

'How?' the steward asked everyone present. 'First she holds the rod of Lenmer'el without harm, now the spear to which every troll is beholden? But you could not wield the sword of black fire, could you?'

'I allowed it,' the shamaness explained regarding the

spear. 'TotoMuru is my ancestor by right of my first marriage. I may not have the right to wield the spear in battle, nor do I ever wish to. The wilful suffering of my kin will never be on *my* conscience.'

The general grunted, it seemed he agreed with her on this point.

She continued, 'As for the sword, it is a troll right. Any of troll blood may wield it, thus she could not. Yet it takes one of the royal line to unlock its full powers… Your half troll here is a royal gift to your people. I would love to know where his mother has gotten to; she has not been seen in some time among our kind since her banishment. She is welcome to return any time she desires, the council has declared it.'

'Let it be the young prince's decision,' King Dunnkan said after a moment of thought. 'But what will you do now there is to be no war?'

Everyone, including all the trolls, looked at the shamaness. She seemed burdened by a great weight, 'I would not be so sure of that as yet, Red King. True, you have nothing to fear from the trolls today or any day coming. But we have seen the omens… the red dusk sinks over your horizon almost every day now. War is coming to the Great Kingdom; you may have every expectation of that.'

The room was solemn in her words.

'We are grateful the trolls have chosen to honour the treaties of three hundred years ago,' King Dunnkan said,

        By Dr Joe Ireland

being very tactful about it.

She grunted. 'You gave us no trespass, no injury… you have done well, Red King of men: patient as a hunter.'

All the trolls grunted their agreement.

'We do have one request, however,' she looked at the troll king, and he grunted. The general waved towards the liturgist and beast master, who went to a large stone box that they had carried in here. They moved it forward, but did not open it.

'The greenflame sabre,' the shamaness decreed.

The effect on the room was electric. The steward gasped, and the captain stepped forward to guard the king.

King Dunnkan stood. 'You have … no greater treasure to be won from the field of battle! Why?'

This time, the troll general spoke, 'This causes nothing but contention among us. War, and violence. I don't think it cursed, at least not yet. But it is a token of power that we trolls cannot keep our pride from. Too many will die to claim it, and any who do, will likely only want to achieve what Ki-Tieri almost did. You, and we, do not want that again.'

The king nodded, and four of his guards quickly moved to take the stone box away.

'I… have no words to sufficiently thank you for this… profound token of peace!' He admitted. 'We will return it to the High Kingdom immediately.'

The shamaness huffed rudely, 'If you're an idiot. Look

how good a job they did keeping it from us last time!'

King Dunnkan merely smiled, and winked. It was clear to Kialessa that he had no intention of getting the sword back to the Great Kingdom, but if everyone thought it was going back then they'd all be looking the wrong place.

The shamaness chuckled. Then she sighed. 'Well! If that concludes our discussion, we beg your leave, Red King.'

King Dunnkan paused before replying. 'I don't know what to say… thank you. Thank you for … thank you for the part you have played in meaning we are alive today, and that both our people are at peace.'

She nodded at him, in a very human way.

King Dunnkan walked down, into arms reach of the heavily armed trolls. No one moved. Then, the ageing human reached out his hand to the leader of the council of troll kings. 'To peace,' he offered.

The troll king looked at his hand, and gently took it, speaking in Emerellian, 'To peace...'

They shook hands, and then the troll king stepped up and pressed his enormous forehead to King Dunnkan's brow. The troll king closed his eyes, his face a picture of reverence and respect. 'To peace, and understanding between our two very different peoples.'

'Agreed,' the king of men agreed, and they parted.

***

 By Dr Joe Ireland

It didn't matter how relieved Kialessa was feeling, neither the king nor the shamaness would allow her any time to rest. Instead they taught her but one phrase in the troll language of the shamaness.

Piex explained it means, 'This is the spear that killed the tyrant. I was holding this spear when it killed the tyrant.'

Kialessa and Eclipse then spent the next two days riding north and then back again, displaying the spear to every troll war camp they came across. The spear, it was obvious, had a will of its own. Usually it would imbed itself in the soil in the centre of the meeting place, where the priest and warriors could stroke it for strength and good luck. It seemed happy enough to be carried by her. But never, not even once, did she feel like she owned it in any way.

It was the wife's. It had always been.

And everywhere they went, trolls celebrated. They had never asked for war. Some were disappointed, slinking away with bitter looks, still sharpening their swords. But none dared challenge the shamaness, or the little tae'anaryn of the Great Kingdom who had slain the greatest warlord since TotoMuru.

And still, Ki-Taieri proved an unworthy shadow.

Everywhere they went, a new call came up, 'See, see! Even their children can defeat our king! We cannot go to war against the Great Kingdom, it will mean death and pain and misery for us! Return to the land that owns you!

Return to the land that owns you!'
There would be peace.

11 I was holding the spear that killed the tyrant

***

Kialessa had to admit the pack up was undeniably less hasty than their arrival, the entire area cleared by the time they returned. The king set up a remembrance stone for the war that had never happened, with the names of each and every solider engraved on it – with Eclipse and her

          By Dr Joe Ireland

own name in the places of greatest honour.

The trolls provided some hefty supplies for their journey, and they gave them some magically hardened wooden axes, as strong as steel, and bone daggers and hessian tents as a gift. The trolls asked nothing but the chance to return their armies to their lands in peace, but King Duncan insisted they keep the small chest of treasures.

'I can't believe we survived,' Piex muttered. He sounded almost disappointed, as though death were just another experiment for him to try.

'I'm just glad we get baked taters again,' Posk grinned.

'You may have to hold up a week on those potatoes,' Allastassia mocked him in good friendship. 'You'll never guess where we're headed next. Any guesses?'

'Don't bore us,' Eclipse demanded dryly.

Allastassia ignored her, and continued cheerfully. 'Your uncle's old place, Piex. The "Far Keep" they're calling it now!'

Eclipse unfolded her arms, 'Really? Well, I might stick around for that then. Might be fun to see where I grew up again. Did you humans drain the swamp?'

'They drained the swamp,' Darrix informed her.

Eclipse huffed, 'Pity, I liked the swamp. Full of life and colour and … *scents*. But I suppose the biting insects were a bother and all. That, and you *don't* want my father ever returning.

'He's not been seen or heard of since,' Allastassia

informed them all. 'We keep no treasure there, and there's barely a score of men to man the tower.'

'And it was the first official confirmation of the troll hoard massing at the Broadwaters, so it's paying for itself,' Darrix added.

Eclipse huffed. Lost in thought for a moment, 'He might return, as a point of pride. But I think his love was tied up in the work of Tobiuus. Wherever the wizard goes, the dragon will soon follow, I expect.'

Piex looked up at her and nodded, seeming to indicate that he'd already come to that conclusion.

'And...' Allastassia seemed to have having a rare moment of social anxiety, 'what will you do once we get back to the kingdom, Eclipse?'

She glared at the enchantress, 'So keen to get rid of me, Allastassia!'

Allastassia held her ground, but did not argue.

Eclipse let out a breath. 'I don't know. I just... I don't know...'

***

Kialessa found the trip back in genuinely pleasant, apart from the simmering discontent of a moulting dragon. In either form, her skin was clearly peeling now. She picked at it almost constantly unless someone showed they noticed.

She could have flown away at any time, but she simply

     By Dr Joe Ireland

did not.

The trip took a week. The change in the wizard's tower was noticeable; for one, it was clean. The garrison has gone double time to make the place look good. There were new locks on all the doors, and the stairs and windows all in good repair. The swamp was dry, with some well ploughed land now budding new wheat by the entrances. Best of all, no goblins in any directions.

It looked good.

Eclipse went in, sniffed at it with great derision, and then went down to the basement and pointed out a secret entrance no one had blocked up yet. She walked into her mother's old cell, now cleaned and empty. She'd looked at it for quite some time, then walked out without saying a word.

'Tare that prison cell apart and fill it with stone,' the captain ordered the garrison.

If Eclipse had heard, she said nothing.

A week and a half later, by the time they'd reached the castle of Lenmer'el, there was a huge celebration ready for them. People lined the streets the entire way up, and every solider was greeted with hugs and tears. None few offered up prayers to the gods, for not a single soldier had died in the war that never happened.

The meal went on for half a day, the jesters being put to the task. It was a happy, noisy affair.

For all, except the silent, sullen human form dragon that sat by Kialessa's side and said nothing till late in day.

She sat there, ignoring everyone, and everything, when she suddenly sat bolt upright and started sniffing the air.

'What is it?' Kialessa asked.

Eclipse turned to face the king, and without any manners spoke to him as though he was just any other man, 'Is that a platinum fork?' she asked him.

He had only just picked it up to get himself some of the newly offered meats. 'Indeed, it is,' he said with a grin. He was clearly enjoying the celebration.

'May I have it?' Eclipse asked.

Everyone at the table had noticed now, but the room was still a din.

King Dunnkan shrugged, and placed the fork in her outstretched hand.

She sniffed it, rubbed it against her nose, and bit the end clean off.

The queen gasped, and the room fell silent.

Nothing could be heard except for the dim crunching of solid metal in the young girl's mouth. 'Mmmm,' she muttered, the first contented sound in weeks. '*Delicious.*'

Everyone looked at her, but she didn't even seem to notice. Once she'd finished the fork, she looked up at the rest of the king's cutlery, a forlorn look of silent pleading.

The king grinned, and looked over at his captain.

Bon Shur'e, captain of the king's guard, leant over the table and gently whispered, 'Come with me, young dragon.'

He motioned to Kialessa as well, and she ran down to

     By Dr Joe Ireland

drag Eclipse away from her forlorn gaze at the platinum knife in the king's hand with a pitiful whine. For reasons unknown, Posk decided he was coming along as well.

The four of them walked around the castle in the night. The captain grabbed a torch to light his way, but none of the youth needed any. Actually, it was a bit of a distraction to Kialessa. Shadow beings were rare, even more so in the castle grounds. Kialessa liked trying to spot the shadow beasts of the Shadowrealm every time she explored the castle, but the flickering light made it impossible tonight.

'Where are we going?' Kialessa dared to ask. She was getting braver.

'Wait and see,' he replied.

They walked on. Eclipse could not stop scratching her nose; it was getting all scuffed up.

Finally, they began to ascend the narrow, spiralled staircase of one of the highest towers of the castle. Kialessa was soon out of breath, it was such a steep climb! On and on they went, while the waxing crescent of Lumos the moon grew brighter in the night sky. Posk seemed to have enough energy to make the journey twice.

Finally they made it to a barred and bolted door. The captain inserted his ring, and with a twist dissolved the middle beam. 'It needs a password,' he told them. 'Young child, Eclipse. What would you like your password to be?'

She looked puzzled. 'Why?'

'The room beyond, and all within it, are yours to keep. A gift from the "Red King" for all you did to save our lives, and the lives of a million more in the Great Kingdom beyond.'

She shook her head. 'I did nothing. I just delivered a message.'

'You saved my life, Eclipse.'

She shrugged. 'You have saved mine as well… and… taught me perhaps a little bit about humility.' She sighed. 'But I really did mean it, call the password "why"?'

He looked thoughtful, and nodded. Speaking the word the door opened fully.

Within the room was almost entirely bare stone, with nothing but a single window to let in the light. A fireplace was burning, warming the room quite well. However, it was the pile of silver-coloured coins at least as tall as Kialessa that drew their attention most of all. They gleamed in the moonlight.

Eclipse gave a strange half cheer, half wail of delight and ran right in. She dived onto the pile and ran her hands through the coins. Then she took the biggest piece of platinum she could find, and bit a chunk right off, munching on it like it was chocolate.

'This has my mother's scent all over it,' she muttered between mouthfuls.

Posk picked up a spare coin that had rolled their way. He tried to bite it in half, but quickly gave up on the idea. He rolled it back towards Eclipse who watched its every movement with covetous eyes.

Posk shrugged.

	By Dr Joe Ireland

'No, no,' the captain disagreed, 'All from the royal treasury! Our gratitude to the sky dragons for helping prevent a war.'

'Mgnhfff,' Eclipse showed she disagreed and didn't care all in one inarticulate noise. She just sat there, rubbing the metal all over her cheeks now. 'I know what I have to do.'

Then, with a dramatic flourish, Eclipse jumped out of the pile of coins and turned into a dragon. She gave a fearsome roar, then prowling about she turned and bashed her head against the wall. The tower swayed, but the dragon didn't notice. Then she ran her face down the stones, cutting away a great swathe of skin. 'Hold this!' she ordered Posk, pointing to her moulting pelt, 'and stand your ground!'

He did as he was told. Eclipse the dragon turned around and pulled hard against him. The struggle was real. Eclipse roared, and Posk was yelling. There was a strange taring sound as her dragon skin came loose.

Eclipse stood there, panting with effort. Her skin was pale grey, and looked so very tender. She seemed to have grown a hand or two taller as well. Her claws were stunted and broken, and sweat, or something, glistened over her scales. 'That hurt,' she confessed.

Posk stood there. It looked like he was holding a shrunken and eyeless dragon.

'Keep it, make a vest out of it or something,' Eclipse told him. 'May it protect you from rot, and the cold.'

He nodded, and she half smiled at him as she turned. Then, putting her head down on the stones, she pressed her way along them with her dragon jaw agape. She skirted along the edge of her pile of platinum, seeming to vacuum what must have been several bucket loads right into her mouth. When she sat up, her stomach was visibly distended. 'Oh, yummm,' she said. 'I've needed that for twelve years…'

She began to make herself comfortable, as if ready to sleep. 'Have then bring in pineoak,' she told the captain. 'Fresh logs, new each week. But *do not wake me!*'

'Yes, young dragon.'

She smiled, slamming her head down on her coins. She looked so sleepy! Already, the air began to feel misty, strange swamp lights blinking in and of existence around the tired dragon. 'Kialessa…' she muttered.

Kialessa stood close, and ran her hand along her friend's muzzle.

'You're a good friend. By the time I wake up, you will be a full-grown woman. You might have married, and I will live to see your children! Promise me you will live, so that I can meet your children. Do you promise?'

'I promise,' Kialessa smiled, not sure how she might keep that promise. Suddenly she realised just how long that might be, for her. It was a long time to say goodbye to a good friend. Tears filled Kialessa's eyes.

'Oh, not for me!' Eclipse chided her, trying to use a dragon claw to wipe her face. 'Save your tears for a worthy

     By Dr Joe Ireland

cause – we dragons are **meant** to sleep.'

'I will,' Kialessa promised, but it only seemed to make her even sadder. Eclipse meant well. Eclipse had been though some terrible experiences and still only tried to do what was right. She was going to miss her dragon.

She hugged her, and Eclipse smiled but said nothing. As she laid her large head on the platinum coins a strange scent wafted up from the mound. Dark, green mosses sprung to life around her, and the stones were covered with lichen that should have taken years to form. But the scent was not of the dismal swamp where her father had raised her, but was the life filled ambiance of the abundant wetlands, the scent of a living, running stream that brought life to all it passed.

The dragon was already asleep.

'Woah…' Posk muttered.

The captain indicated they should leave, not daring to speak.

It wasn't easy to say goodbye and lock the door, but Kialessa eventually found a way to do it.

# Let Sleeping Dragons Lie

*Most people don't hate you. And most people don't like you either. They just… wait to see if you're useful to them or not.*

*Aolith, cited in 'Recollections of the tae'anaryl.' 314 CY*

*Until you risk presenting your sincere, vulnerable, and imperfect self to the judgment of an indifferent world, you will never find a place to belong.*

*Bon Sure'e, captain of the king's guard, 313CY*

 By Dr Joe Ireland

Kialessa did not re-join the party, but went instead to the castle parapets, to talk the moon, to ask her to watch over her friend.

The guards ignored her. Perhaps it was because she was a dame? Perhaps it was she was now a hero, for the King had spared no time spreading the shamaness's lies – that Kialessa had somehow slain Ki-Tieri with the spear of the troll warlords. Yet the humans of Lenmer'el seemed far less inclined to believe it than the trolls ever did.

Toward midnight she heard footsteps approaching, bare feet slapping noisily on solid stone. Only Posk sounded like that.

He looked up at her, and she watched the moon. 'They're asking for you, Tauira,' he told her.

She smiled, 'You don't need to call me that any more Posk, I am not your tutor.'

'Yes you are,' he quickly disagreed. He shuffled on the floor, kicking the stones though they did not budge. 'I need… these tall men… I don't get them. Now I have words for what I've always felt. Their "burning" eyes, and they are so tall!'

Kialessa smiled at him. He had no trouble breaking those tall legs on occasion, or punching a "burning" eye! He was just nervous. 'You have nothing to fear from these men,' she told him, really only referring to Darrix.

Posk huffed, and threw his arms onto the parapet to glare out beside her. She had to move away to avoid getting squashed. 'But I couldn't stay with the trolls either.

They're just… and I thought I was rough around the edges. I don't belong there… and I don't belong here.'

'Hmm,' she said not too sure how to disagree.

'So we unbelongers belong with each other,' he informed her with a grin.

She patted his hand. It was a very nice thing to say. Had Posk finally found where he belonged?

He sighed, put his back against the wall, and let his feet slide out from under him till he plonked on the floor. 'I still don't know what the word "prince" means, anyway.'

She sat by him, wondering if this was one of those "give advice" times or "listen to feelings" moments. 'Do you… does anyone know what happened to your parents?'

He looked away, seeming annoyed. 'Mum's out there, in the forest. I go see her every few days. She's glad I "found my way", but doesn't like the headband that lets me speak, and stand like a man. I love this headband! Gotta thank Piex, I keep forgetting to do that! I hope he doesn't want it back one day. I hated having to fight for my life without it. I can't even remember what happened, though sometimes I dream… and Dad… I don't know. I haven't seen him in many days… what's the word for it? Years. I haven't seen him in years.'

'Do you know who he is?'

'Sure. I'll know him soon as I see him. Never knew his name though, I'll have to ask mum next time I'm around. Tell her all about the fight that didn't happen, and the fights that did. She'll like that. She speaks well, you know. Maybe I'll take you to see her sometime. She'll like you.'

Kialessa was quite amazed. She had no idea Posk was… so … normal? Was that the word she wanted?

'She's bit scary when she gets mad though,' Posk admitted.

'Runs in the family?' Kialessa grinned.

'Yeah. My sisters trouble.'

'You have a sister!'

Posk grinned, and looked like it was old news she was supposed to already know. 'My older brother died around the time dad left. My sis is still around, but she won't come up the college. I tried to teach her; she prefers troll things. You'd better be ready to dodge though, she uses a club on all the rabbits and counts anything she doesn't like a rabbit! Ha! That's sis for you! ... But you'd probably better not tell anyone. I don't think the men like having trolls in their lands. It'd be trouble… but if mum ever leaves away, I might never find her again.'

His voice was genuinely sad, as though this was a day he did not look forward to, but could not avoid. She wondered what Posk's early life was like before the men of the city found him and decided to teach him their ways. Did he live in a mud hut under a fallen tree, with nothing but his lonely mother and rabbit squishing sister for company, against a world he could neither name nor explain? It sounded like a rough start.

'I will come, soon. By winter's dawn if not sooner. Next

Planasday-'

'No rush!' he interrupted her.

She decided it would be better to wait till he invited her.

The guards in the tower laughed at some game they were playing. Posk picked up a pebble and threw it away. 'I am no prince of men, and I am no prince of trolls.'

'Oh, I disagree,' she said. 'I saw you hold the sabre of the troll king. You bore it like you owned it.'

'That was pretty excellent,' he admitted. 'Still, where do you think the High King will keep it?'

'It's not going to the High King,' she informed him.

'But I heard them say-'

'More cunning,' she admitted. 'But my guess is it's hidden up in the keep here, probably in the armoury, where Flower and I got my dagger of the dwarven lady.'

He looked confused, 'Oh, your shadow dagger! They have a room full of that stuff? Oh yeah, sounds fun! Ha! ... why would they say they're taking it to the High Kingdom then, whatever that is.'

Kialessa smiled, 'So that people look in the wrong place. That sword is powerful Posk. It almost started a war.'

He still looked confused. 'So you tell them where it isn't... so that they... look in the wrong place! Oh, that's clever! That's how they hide something! Woah... that's lying!'

'Well, sort of. Maybe they intend to take it to the high

king, but since they have to wait for the right moment they can't take it yet.'

'Woah… I can't… that's like lying with a half-truth on top. I can't even keep up with that, my Tauira. See! I still need you to teach me things!'

'That's what friends do, Posk.'

He looked gruff. 'Yeah, friends do … things for friends,' he muttered, looking like he was thinking of his crush Allastassia. 'Makes me wonder,' he said, sitting up. 'I was listening to the dude, what's his name? The guy with all the axes. He was talking the elf, with the pointy hat? You know?'

'The captain of the king's guard and the royal arcanist, the high wizard?'

'Oh, that's their names. All right. Anyway, they're upset about something, something about that the trolls were not the real problem.'

'What do you mean?'

'All right, um, the wizard says the High King is using all this trouble with the trolls as, and I quote, an "excuse" to build up an army of his own. He's ordered something called the draft, and that each nation send down troops to protect his kingdom. They say by the end of next year his forces will be more than ten times the standing army. The captain isn't happy, says he can't see a "need" for it. I don't know what I think. Another fight?'

Though no humans had died this side of the Broadwaters, she was still exhausted, and could only guess what trouble a full-scale war might involve. The night-time fell silent in their wordless vigil of the moonlit sky.

'I guess we'll see soon,' Posk announced.

'I hope not,' Kialessa admitted.



By Dr Joe Ireland

## Teacher notes

This book deals in part with finding your place in the world - where do you think you belong? Is it where you feel safe? Where there are people who understand and care for you? Or where you can contribute and feel needed? What does it *mean* to belong?

Posk and Eclipse's experiences of belonging are contrasted against each other in the book. Posk has no place to belong but manages to fit in almost everywhere, while Eclipse has a place that loves her dearly, but leaves it because she not feel she belongs. Do you agree?

"When we don't feel like we belong—when we feel excluded, rejected, or like an outsider—it saps our precious mental resources and energy, distracts us, and keeps us from being fully present in the moment. For instance, when students feel like they belong, they show more motivation, engagement, and self-efficacy . . . when its lacking, students find it difficult to succeed academically and are less likely to thrive." (Karyn Lewis, "Building Students' Sense of Social Belonging as a Critical First Step, March, 2016 https://educationnorthwest.org/northwest-matters/building-students-sense-social-belonging-critical-first-step)

## Belonging

The first quote is inspired from the following, real world, saying by the author Brené Brown: "Because true belonging only happens when we present our authentic, imperfect selves to the world, our sense of belonging can never be greater than our level of self-acceptance." — Brené Brown, <u>Daring Greatly: How the Courage to Be Vulnerable Transforms the Way We Live, Love, Parent, and Lead</u>

What do you think of Brené's idea? Is it necessary to be sincere and honest to find a place to belong – even if that means admitting your vulnerabilities and fears?

## Three weeks previously

Posk voices our question for this book, "Where do I belong?" Where do you think posk, the half troll, belongs during a war with his mother's people? Where does Eclipse, the daughter of a moon and rot dragon, belong? Where does Kialessa, the 'half soul', though she is an honoured hero of the kingdom of Lenmer'el?

## The army departs

In this chapter we meet some of the people who will be the focus of this adventure; Kialessa, Eclipse, Piex, Darrix and Allastassia.

Why does Posk like to start arguments with Allastassia?

     By Dr Joe Ireland

Why do you think she allows herself to be drawn into the arguments?

What is a 'fiery conflagration'?

## At the front

Kialessa and Eclipse are out on a scouting run when they, and their companion, are attacked. What did they learn once they'd flown so far off route?

Kialessa and Eclipse discuss where Eclipse belongs. The dragon is in a very bad moon in this book, any ideas why? Where does Eclipse think she belongs?

What do you think of Kialessa's claim, "Sometimes it's nice to be helpful, just to know that you can make a difference."

## Diplomacy

Does Kialessa feel she belongs here? How does she know? Does she have friends to care for, important jobs to do, and people in authority who show trust and affection towards her? How do these things help her feel like she belongs? What is she doing, even without noticing it, to make sure she feels like she belongs.

What do you think the phrase, "Knowledge without purpose is a bitter well," means? When water is 'bitter' when it cannot be drunk, and is useless for helping people feel less thirsty.

Eclipse is going through a tough time – how might you help a dragon friend who is tired, confused, and ready to take of their skin and have a nap for a few years?

## The battle

In this chapter, the dragons of the sky grant the humans of Lenmer'el an easy victory. Why do you think the trolls weren't willing to fight once they saw the vision?

However, there can be internal battles every bit as challenging as those ones that threaten our homes and families. Why does Eclipse feel unwelcomed at home? Do you think that people are being unwelcoming towards her, or is she just taking their kindness for granted? What does Eclipse want?

## The training

The captain's words at the end of the chapter here echo the thoughts of Brené Brown from the start of the book. Do you think Eclipse was able to get to know herself, and where she belongs, better by being sincere, and coming to know her limits – even if she did pick a fight she couldn't win? Can failure really be one of life's greatest teachers, teaching Eclipse lessons about her limits that she would never learn any other way?

## Dirt and ultimatum

What do you think of the phrase "One does not **find** where they belong. They **create** it... and then they create themselves in the image of it." Do you think you can have an influence in making the place and gathering the people that will help you feel you belong? And once you create/find such a place, do you find change some things about who you are in order to try and fit in?

Once more, Kialessa finds herself kidnapped. What does the troll king intend to do with her and her friends? What should she do?

## The prince

So, Posk is the son of an exiled princess. What do you think? Once the trolls realise this they decide he belongs with them. Do



By Dr Joe Ireland

you agree? Is it wise to choose to belong somewhere just because you are welcomed there, or your family grew up there? Is that what it means to belong? What might life be like for Posk if he chooses to live with the trolls from now on?

## The visitor

Imagine you were trapped in prison cage, what one gift would you wish for? A way to escape perhaps? What significance do you think there might be in the king's gifts to the prisoners?

Why do you think Eclipse is still helping out after she promised she was leaving because no one wanted her?

## And all troll fealty

In this chapter, the troll warlord Ki-Tieri is keen to prove that he is worthy of being their king. He has their most famous weapons, the hand of their queen in marriage, and has called them all to war. Does this make him worthy to be their king? What does it take to make a worthy king?

Do the people belong to their king, or does the king belong to his people?

## He who sings

Why didn't Eclipse stay, and why did Kialessa – even though there was great danger?

The quote at the start of the chapter asks us to think about accepting love into our hearts from those who would ask us to belong. Do we sometimes reject kind words and deeds from others simply because it does not fit with our image of who we are?

How did Piex survive the troll trial? What does this make you think about the trolls?

## She who dances

The quote: "Be yourself – everyone else is already taken." Is from the great American author and comedian Oscar Wilde. What do you think it means? What is it trying to teach us about belonging?

How does Allastassia use her talents to win the trolls hearts? Do you think she could have fought her way out instead?

How will Darrix survive, or is there no hope for him?

## The sacrifice

What is Darrix plan for survival? Do you like it? Did you think it might have worked to stop a war, or was it never really an option given the troll king's goals?

The troll king demands; "bring all the children of our enemies to the hill of trial *right now*. I challenge them all to the sacred right of rulership." In what way is this a careless challenge? Who else might count as 'the children of our enemies'?

## The hill of trial

It was hard to imagine a battle scene where a powerful, skilled, trained warrior could be beaten by 6 school kids. In the end, what do you think *really* defeated the warlord Ki-Taieri?

Perhaps you did not notice, but Ki-Taieri was looking for a place to belong in this whole story as well – as the king who finally defeated the Great Kingdom. What did he do to create himself in the image of what he believed his role as king meant? Do you think he would have made a good king?

Arguably, Jindalessa knew where she belonged the whole story through. But rather than try and force her people to accept her for who she wanted to be, she served them and cared for them – even if it meant making great personal sacrifices for



By Dr Joe Ireland

herself. Is this what it takes to belong? At what point does sacrificing your goals for others in order to belong become insincere, and result in them accepting you for something you don't actually want to be?

## End to war

Kialessa doesn't lie, but she lets other people believe the lie that she killed Ki-Taieri and not Jindalessa through her priestess powers. Should she insist they tell the more accurate truth? Or is it wiser to let them think a child was able to slay their rising king in order to stop a war?

Kialessa, Piex and Eclipse get to visit the tower where they were prisoners earlier this year. What has changed?

Finally, Eclipse gets the dragon sleep that she's needed for a long, long time. When do you think she might wake up? What might it be like to have a friend you didn't see for ten years or more, what might change? Does Eclipse finally have a place to belong? Does Posk?

## Let sleeping dragons lie

Sometimes we'd like to just leave things as they are… like sleeping dragons.

But sometimes silent trouble is brewing, ready to explode into violence when we least expect it. Dragons are famous for being upset if you wake them up too early. It can mean big trouble to wake up a sleeping dragon …

Posk admits to overhearing the captain complaining that, even without a troll war, the High King is dramatically increasing his army. It is like a 'sleeping dragon', a huge army waiting around with nothing to do, or is the High King aware of dangers he's still not telling anyone about? What trouble could be brewing behind the scenes, deep underground, ready to burst into violence when the good people of Lenmer'el least expect it – as if someone has awoken  sleeping dragon…

## *Suggestions*

Workshop ways in which you can help others to feel accepted in social situations:

1. Use people's names, esp. their preferred name.
2. Give, and take on, important tasks that help others. Getting the scissors for the group project helps others to realise you want to be included.
3. Don't use jokes that degrade the race, religion, etc., of the people you want to include. Laugh a little at other people's jokes, even if it's only to help them feel accepted.
4. Smile, use eye contact.
5. What can you suggest?

These are some of the very things you can do to help yourself feel accepted in a new social group!

            By Dr Joe Ireland

# Trolls

The following brief treatise I present to you, good master De'Feur, in gratitude for your magnanimous tutelage, to which I may justly ascribe in large part at having protected me and many others from death and deprivation at the hands of the would-be troll hoard invasion of 313CY. I fear I have little to add to what you already known about troll history, culture, and biology, yet am so astonished at the lack of knowledge thus far presented hereunto in writing that I cannot not but add to what is as yet so poorly understood of trolls. Here is a summary of my understanding and beliefs as thus far attained;

## Timeline

- -30CY. According to the troll lore, the troll that would become their great war chief TotoMuru (Called TotoRore by many troll historians) was captured as a young troll from his native lands among the Sahani'ea and forced to work in Emerel under the most depraved and dehumanising of conditions. This is to be contrasted with the history humans tell that he was born and raised in Emerel as an educated servant. The truth is likely somewhere between the two extremes, both representing the diverse experiences of trolls in the pre-Emerellian human civilisation. This injustice and inequality being a major contributing factor to the rejection of slavery as legal in Emerel today, and a cause of the troll uprising of the time.

- -10 CY. The story is told that TotoMuru escaped his human captors and returned to his homeland with tales of troll suffering and exploitation among the humans. After inspiring his home tribe to rise up against the humans and reclaim the stolen slaves, he claims the chieftainship by rite of single-handed combat. Records differ if he was born nobility or earned it.

- -9 CY the following year the 22-year-old troll chieftain sends messages to the local tribes of Sahani'ea to inform them of his plans. Some flock to his call, the others are swiftly cajoled using his rapidly gaining military power. He adopts a practice that the longer a tribe holds out in subscribing to his cause, the worse treatment they can expect in his army. Trolls admit he even wiped out several clans entirely that refused to submit. Within a year the entire nation is gearing up for war.

- -8 CY knowing it would take the entire troll hoard

    By Dr Joe Ireland

to win such a battle, TotoMuru sends entire legions of armed forces into the other troll's nations. They swiftly put down any resistance and demand trolls everywhere come to the battle, forcing loosely held coalitions of tribes to declare themselves strongly united nations or face conquest by the Sahani'ea. This great time of unification saw a meteoric rise in trade and science among the trolls. This is point at which whispers begin among the Emerellians of 'trouble in the troll lands', which almost no one takes any care about.

- -5 CY TotoMuru and his forces begin serious preparations for war. They build roads leading to their planned invasion regions, and prepare massive machines for war. Spies are cited regularly in the disparate and separate nations of the Great Kingdom (who are still only loosely allied at this time).

- -2 CY. The invasion begins. The first three nations in his path are the dwarves of the Feuerdrache , the Perliou elves, and the human lands of Emerel itself (after traversing the wilderness that would become our nation of Nomer'el a hundred years later). Rather than trying to concur the nearby nations, giving the further nations time to prepare, in a military manoeuvre most would later consider genius he divides his forces into three massive hoards and ploughs them through every nation and kingdom in the West and instead concurs the nations in the East – plundering as they go. Each nation still bears the scar of the ravaging trolls, and a huge amount of treasure has yet (and will likely never be) recovered from troll hands. I myself have hefted some of the weapons and a crown from a slain human prince that the trolls once claimed as "payment" for centuries of enslavement at human and other nation's hands. The troll hoards attack the Eastern nations of the blithlings, giants, and terranoid – each race having a similar advance as trolls do when it comes to commands of elements, in particular; sand, stone and earth. He enslaves these races, thus placing all other nations between two very wealthy and now well-equipped troll hoards.

- -1 CY inspired by tales of easy plunder and swift victory, trolls surge into the war grounds. Troll sages readily admit that the trolls commit a key tactical error around this time, ignoring important military targets for softer, more easily plundered, ones. This gives time for the hard targets to get even harder as they dig in for war and rescue survivors from farming districts – now keen to add their contribution against troll hoards. By the end of the year trolls are starting to notice the tide rise against them, and some losses of poorly defended assets are noted here.

- 1CY (technically 0CY but it's impossible to convince non-wizards of this), an army led by the ex-farmer Emerel wins a key battle against the local troll warlord, effectively liberating Emerel from troll control. As livid as TotoMuru is about this – seeking human lands above all else, he plays a patient game and focuses on strengthening his hold on the East. Leaving the retaking of

        By Dr Joe Ireland

Emerel to lesser generals is, again, seen as a meteoric error, but an understandable one in the context of the sheer size of the war and everything TotoMuru was trying to achieve in a very short time. Soon thereafter, at an undisclosed venue, Emerel convenes a conclave of all the seventeen nations threated by destruction at troll hands, uniting them in the cause of freedom under his personal banner. Vital military and weaponry information begins to be shared openly among the heavily beleaguered nations.

- 2CY While two other nations fall to the troll hoards, concerted efforts are made to hinder and occasionally stall troll transit through the three invasion corridors. Plunder almost ceases to tempt more trolls to the invasion, while new recruits are forced to wait until a large troll hoard can come and get them. The Great Kingdom develops reliable tactics and weaponry to hold the hoard back.

- 3CY officially, trolls are no longer gaining territory in the Great Kingdom. The invasion corridors close completely except for massive incursions, which are carefully watched, counted, and hindered. Trolls begin to become frustrated, and food supplies dwindle. The Great Kingdom is better prepared for the coming famine, while trolls are very cautious about spreading out enough to raise crops, especially in lands generally unfamiliar to them.

- 4CY. Several key troll losses are noted at this time, and while the Great Kingdom loses much, the unprepared trolls are still dying at a faster rate. The Troll council convenes and asks TotoMuru to abandon the war, he ignores them. Emerel is declared king of the human nation that takes his name, and forge the crown of the King.

- 5CY. Emerel and TotoMuru finally meet on the field of battle. Expecting an easy victory against the devastated nation, TotoMuru's forces are decimated by the king and his crown – Emerel turns the power of the spear of TotoMuru against him, by using the power of the crown to directly attack TotoMuru with such vigour and ferocity that his entire hoard is wounded and driven back or face annihilation. Trolls nationwide dig in for conflict. They hold their lands, but no longer enlarge their wins from around this point on. The troll council convenes again, begging TotoMuru to leave the war. He threatens their lives. Again, at the end of the year, the council dares beg him once more, and he declares the death oath. That night, he is slain by one of his own people, the serving maid.

- 6CY the dawn of the new year reveals TotoMuru dead in his tent. Trolls abandon their posts in an almost organised retreat. Elves, dwarves and humans eventually blockade the retreating trolls and demand all slaves captured in the war be returned in exchange for safe passage of the remaining trolls. The troll council, already safely ensconced in troll lands, readily agrees, sending back almost all the slaves and a fair amount of plunder back as well, as a "good will" gesture. Humans confess

　　　　　By Dr Joe Ireland

the enslavement of trolls was unjust, but do not go so far as to call the invasion and plundering justified. Several hardened troll outposts refuse to leave; most are besieged and eventually destroyed.

• Today, 313CY: Trolls are no longer treated as slaves in the Great Kingdom, and they enjoy a growing acceptance as traders and mercenaries. Most are wary, however, and evidence of the decimation of the troll hoards three hundred years ago is still readily in evidence – many towns and castles have yet to be rebuilt. Several troll holdings and fortresses built during the war are still in ready use in the Great Kingdom today, as is most of the works used to protect the citizens there from marauding troll hoards. It will be noted that some assets, such as the Mountain Bridge Fortress in giant lands is still entirely a troll abode, though they no longer claim obedience to the trolls of the West.

# Troll biology

Without meaning to seem disrespectful, trolls face challenges unique to their race.

**Height/Intelligence conundrum:** To put it simply, as trolls get physically stronger through exercise or nature, their bones grow as well. Thus, getting physically stronger also makes trolls taller. However, for reasons not yet fully understood, the taller a troll is, inevitably, the stupider they become.

Thus the tallest and most physically powerful of all trolls are entirely dolts, incapable of all but rudimentary thought. Some manage a semblance of sentience, attempting to threaten meals from passer-by at a bridge, as legend well attests.

Consequently, the most insightful and intelligent of trolls, with a wisdom that is truly formidable, are inevitably short – some most curiously so. None are smaller than a human child, but their cunning is not to be underestimated, and is rarely fully appreciated even by their taller, more physically powerful kings and leaders.

Tragically, some trolls have taken to concocting a nefarious brew made from human blood that apparently allows them to continue to gain even enormous physical strength without gaining in height, thus avoiding the enstupidification that curses their race.

**Long arms:** Trolls have very large arms for their height, making their physical reach an important factor in battle. Foes have often underestimated the distance of a troll strike – when expecting a glancing blow to their shield find they instead are confronted with a jarring blow to the centre of the shield, or the reach of a troll spear being only a hand further than a human, may still turn a wounding blow into a killing one.

 By Dr Joe Ireland

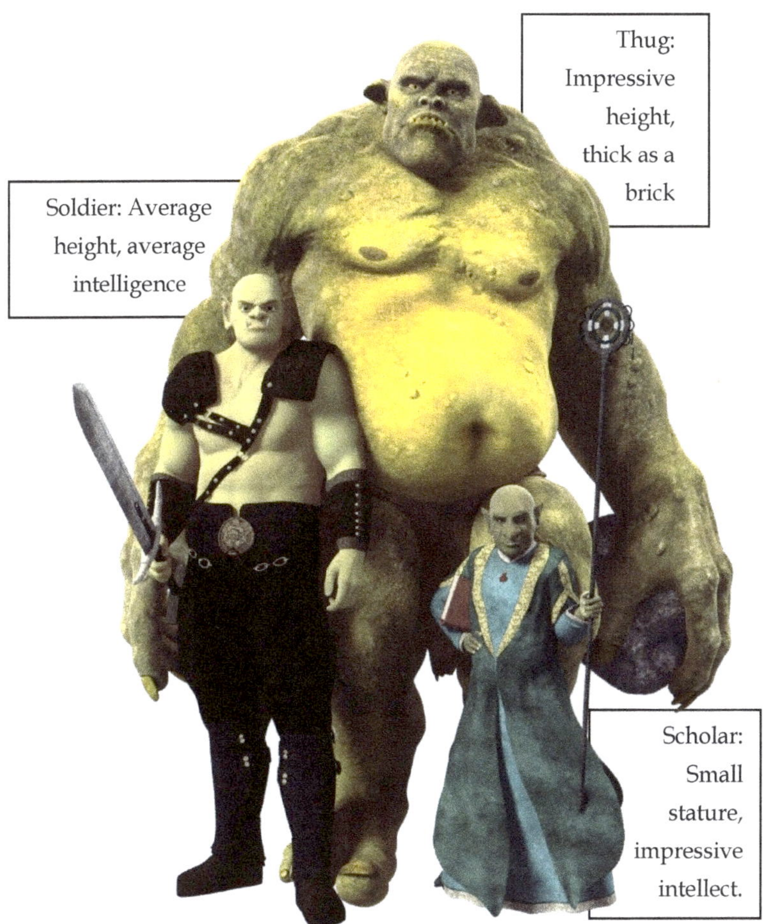



12 Troll height/intelligence conundrum = the taller they are, the stupider they become

**Physical strength:** While it is already well established that trolls rely on physical strength and power to attack, they lack general physical constitution. This is not that their staying power should not be understated; they are formidable warriors in every condition. However, their increased weight and bulk mean they tire a little sooner than other races, and tend to fight in frenetic bursts of power frequently punctuated by slower moments of catching their breath, compared to others.

Some trolls are able to enter a sacred state referred to as their 'troll rage', which grants them even greater physical power at the expense of raw exhaustion afterwards. They have been known to faint outright after raging. Training appears to mitigate such factors.

**Troll healing:** All trolls are reputed to have a very rapid rate of healing, recovering from most wounds in only a day or two. Occasionally one in every a thousand or so has such magnificent healing that some wounds seal in an instant, and heal in only moments. Having witness such healing it is truly astonished, rivalling even the faith of the good priestess of Lenmer'el pace for pace. It does, however, appear limited by other delitriations such as poison or curses.

## Troll magic

The science of wizardry was little known or understood among the trolls at the beginning of the great war, and post war several tribes made the mistake of assuming mere wizardry was a token or item of divine power, and started worshipping both wizard and the tools they used. Such cults have seen less and less favour in the coming centuries, thankfully.

A result of the Great War and the second demon war, there has been a noted rise in the scholar class among the

 By Dr Joe Ireland

trolls. While less popular and understood by their peers, they have nevertheless proven their usefulness on many occasions. As with most wizardry, individuals of extreme intellect can be found, and certain aspects of troll wizardry are yet to be duplicated by any individuals in the Great Kingdom combined. This includes beguiling magic to match the most cunning elven enchanters, and earth summoning powers no terranoid has ever boasted of.

In either event, troll sages still fail to accrue the interest their work frequently deserves, and more effort must be given to attend their accomplishments in the sciences of magic and arithmetic.

## Troll religion

The trolls worship a pantheon of deity as diverse as their own culture. I have managed to distil a few key principals that I hope may aid the genuine seeker of accurate information.

## Ahi

Possibly most accurately translated as either 'breath' or 'honour', Ahi is a mystical property that all beings, deeds and locations possess. Great warriors and leaders have more Ahi, scavengers and thieves have little. One can gain or grow their Ahi via great deeds, or simply remaining in a venue rich with Ahi – what we might refer to as a 'holy site'. This mystical power can be used to control nature, or the minds of trolls and beasts.

Each nation calls it a different name and attribute different qualities, Sahani'ea downplaying the importance of the energy, and the Ohi elevating it to the breath of their creator deity and thus governing daily functions of everyday life.

Most curiously, the Mana'i'oa also speak of gaining Ahi by eating certain body parts of fallen adversaries, and while quite a stock of decorum exists around the practice, still equates to cannibalism. Ki Taieri was keen to make the practice law among all troll nations, which was another source of division among his followers.

## Deity

Trolls worship thousands of deities, having a peculiarly familiar attitude towards many of them, perhaps since most trolls trace their personal heritage to a deified ancestor somewhere. They believe deity need to be appeased, but they are not all to be obeyed. I mention five deities as common among the tribes, however, they usually have a different name and history among each tribe. I am not sure if the deity here mentioned are actually avatars of the deity of the Great Kingdom, as is commonly ascribed by our scholars, but I will attempt to make suggestions where possible.

*Tihi (Ti-hi) – creator deity, god of the rain and water.*

In most stories, Tihi is the uncreated entity that spawned reality from his toenail because he got bored of sitting around in forever, alone. Once the world was made, he lost interest in it after a time, moving on to other interests it is assumed. Only among the Ohi is "Tia'inhi" called upon in daily life as an observant being who

     By Dr Joe Ireland

requires strict obedience to ritual and rites. Some parallels may thus be observed between him and Halm.

*Amaneiha (Ah-ma-ne-ih-ha) – mother deity, of tribe and song.*

Amaneiha, mother deity of fertility, prosperity, family, and cultural song and dance. She is rarely addressed out of respect as the 'great mother of all that lives'. She nevertheless has high expectations of mutual respect, respect for community leaders and the aged, and values skills in hunting, gathering and housebuilding. It is by her will that all houses among the trolls are round. Among the Sahani'ea and Takaniki she is also an earth deity. She seems most similar to Mya.

*Imi – god of battle, streams, and rivers.*

Once a kind a dutiful daughter (son in some mythologies) Imi rose up in rebellion against injustices (usually having suffered at the hand of her divine siblings) and slew them all. The god now is called upon to honour every war, seeking justice or, more commonly, revenge. Imi also provides food and plunder for all warriors, but is curiously also called on in family settings for domestic chores such as washing dishes. Imi may be an avatar or parallel to Annas. It is probably important to note that the Mana'i'oa serving girl who slew TotoMuru was a close follower of Imi.

*Wark – embodiment of lightning.*

Sounding suspiciously like Pikal, Wark relishes conflict, strife, and battle. While of divine parentage in all troll societies, he is less a deity are more the embodiment of lightning itself. He seems willing to work with trolls only when their deeds meet his own ends, and is a loyal friend to no one.

*Dadu – shapechanging trickster demigod of rain and sky.*

The exploits of Dadu are so numerous and chaotic it leaves the thoughtful scholar to wonder if this was one individual, or several. Perhaps the folklore has grown around what was once a real individual, it is difficult to say.  General claims state that he is the originator of practical jokes, and of storytime around the campfire. They say he had a magical hooked spear given him by the gods that allowed him to, among other things; make rain from clouds stolen from the belly button lint of a sky god, invent banana's by slaying a snake and burying its intestines, and flatulating with such potence as to slay an entire demon hoard. Whatever the truth of such matters, Dadu is considered a kind of 'big brother' who looks out for kind-hearted and loyal folks, but will get you into trouble if you slack off or try to rely on him too much.

## Troll society

Trolls live in five distinct groupings known also as nations or cultures. Each nation is divided into thousands of separate tribes of anywhere from a small family group, to tens of thousands in large villages. A troll army is called a hoard.

Trolls typically live a modified hunter / gatherer society mixed with some simple agriculture. Once a family claims an area they rarely move unless necessity forces

		By Dr Joe Ireland

them to. However, trolls are well known for trading, and some are willing to walk for months to trade. A tribe among the Sahahi'ea, for instance, annually make a five month walk all the way to a sister tribe among the Mana'i'oa - and they walk all the way there and back again.

## Troll weaponry

**Hardened wood** – particularly popular among the Ohi, many troll weapons are made quite entirely out of wood. Deadly enough against flesh and bones, the trolls discovered a way to make the wood as hard and sharp as rare blithling steel during the blood war. Axes, shields and spears are all commonly used, and are in no way inferior to their steel counterparts in human lands.

**Toothed weapons** – rather than affix their clubs with metal spikes as the human and dwarves might, trolls have been known to use bone such as monster teeth. Such weapons are believed to contain a portion of the animal's power, and having witnessed them in action I am readily convinced. Non magical varieties, while dangerous, often shatter and are good for a single combat only.

**Hooked weapons** – trolls are fond of affixing hooks to their clubs, allowing them to impale, trip, and disarm foes more readily with a single-handed weapon. They, like the humans, elves and dwarves, have hooked spears and glaives – although once again they are more often made of wood.

**Ranged combat** – it is curious to note that trolls rarely use bows or crossbows, though they are available. Trolls seem to prefer thrown weapons, perhaps because they are more readily able to add their own physical strength to the projectile. Examples include throwing clubs, axes, knives, spears, and slings. Generally, however, trolls prefer to close for close combat and leave distance combat up to their priests, wizards, or artillerists. Most thrown weapons are roped for ease of recovery, and presumably to leave gaping wounds in their enemies.

# Geography

Having never travelled among the trolls, I rely only on their personal reports. They speak of living in a sea of green - endless forests growing above sheer mountains and hidden valleys. The five troll nations line up north to sound along the western edge of the continent claimed predominantly by the Great Kingdom, though the Ohi and Mana'i'oa share an east-western border.

# 5 troll nations

## Sahani'ea (Sa-HA-ni-eh-ah)

The northernmost tribe, the Sahani'ea are respected as fierce warriors.

### Nature

Positioned as the northernmost tribe, the Sahani'ea lands are perhaps the fiercest. Wild and rugged valleys, covered with thick vegetation and constant heat and rain define the nation. To the north, the hot, humid air arriving from the maelstrom mix with the southernmost edge of

          By Dr Joe Ireland

the Poissonvert, resulting in a daily deluge possibly unmatched anywhere on Mya. This results in their lands being filled with huge, humid rainforests that must seem to stretch for journeys in every direction. Rising from the east in a veritable wall of rock and stone, the now impassable mountain range of the dwarven nations prevents the trolls from further expansion. To the west, the mountain waves of the maelstrom prevent almost all fishing, and certainly prevent any serious exploration. To the south, a massive cliff drops down to the Nuingi lands, the warm humid air forming a valley of clouds all year along that the Sahani'ea almost never dare cross.

*Demographics*

Exact numbers are difficult to extract from troll sages, who readily admit a lack of written records will always inhibit an accurate census. However, the Sahani'ea claim between 45-55 separate language groups, divided into thousands of family groups. Troll numbers are estimated between 800,000 and 1.2 million.

In addition to their brute forces, the Sahani'ea contribute some respectable wizardry and sound scholarship as well.

*Government*

Self-governed as tribes, the Sahani'ea looked forward to the arrival of TotoMuru's first horde – as they wanted a troll v's troll fight. Diplomatically, TotoMuru turned up, pointed east, and apparently told them; "The big fight is in that direction" and that was that. Sahani'ea tribes elected a local king, and the rest is history. Now the Sahani'ea government runs as a parliamentary system, however, only tribal chiefs are allowed to vote.

# *Nuingi (Nu-ING-ee)*

### *Overview*

The easy lifestyle of the abundant lands of the Nuingi has given them a reputation as romancers and musicians, and occasionally, rascals.

### *Nature*

Given the tropical climate, the fertile planes and frequent rains make the Nuingi lands comfortable almost all year along. Deep, rich forests of palm trees, with veritable islands of abundance make it easy to find food at any time. To the north a massive cliff makes access to Sahani'ea lands difficult, and an even higher cliff of trees now prevents access to elven lands to the east. A great river divides them from the Takaniki to the south, and the western sea is still very treacherous this close to the maelstrom.

Beasts of the Nuingi are highly magical and often very dangerous. The Atua-haka is seen most often in these lands, and is believed to be native to the region, though there are oral records of its presence in all troll lands.

### *Demographics*

The easy lifestyle of the Nuingi deceived the elves into not considering the trolls any serious threat until much too late. Ruins of ancient origin may be found here, their disproportionate renown perhaps due to greater exploration from human and elven explorers. Travellers sometimes speak of strange cults, given to worshipping magic and even stranger things, noted here.

To the horde, the Nuingi brought powerful masters of music and enchantments, with mystical powers not witnessed before in Emerel.

### Government

The Nuingi didn't see a need for a centralised government even after TotoMuru threatened them with extinction. However, a council of chiefs' act in the roll of a proper kingdom.

# Takaniki (Ta-ka-NI-ki)

### Overview

With a fascination for machinery and magic, the Takaniki are a formidable people.

### Nature

The sub-tropical climate is warm in summer, cool in winter. To the west the great sea lies, rains from the maelstrom making their way into the local lands all year around. The east is the divided from human lands by the Broadwaters river and swamplands, and the unpopulated lands between there and the castle of Lenmer'el proper. A major tributary of the Broadwaters to the north defines their boarder with Nuingi, and a natural ravine, known as the Wound of Amani'e'a (Ah-ma-ni-EH-ah), divides their lands from the Ohi to the southwest and Mana'i'oa south east.

### Demographics

Boasting an army of over 250,000, it is estimated that the trolls of Takaniki number in at close to 1 million. To the horde they contribute considerable magical and machinery might, including self-constructing bridges and bracelets capable of emitting a sound that can not only break apart small buildings, but also sunder magical effects such as the *fiery conflagration*.

### Government

Just prior to TotoMuru's conquest of troll lands, the king of a large Takaniki tribe acquired a powerful staff of stone and fire from would-be human conquerors, which he systematically turned against his fellow tribes until they accepted his government.

This made it easy for TotoMuru to subjugate the nation. Once the powerful Mana'i'oa had given their allegiance to TotoMuru he was able to appear immune to their powerful bracelets weapon, further convincing the Takaniki he was undefeatable.

# Ohi (O-hi)

### Overview

Abundant living allows the Ohi time to consider deeper spiritual things.

*Nature*

The warm, sub-tropical climate, combined with troll commitment to live in harmony with nature, again makes it easy for trolls to live here. They tend to spend a lot of time contemplating or simply enjoying life.

To the northeast the Takaniki lands are separated by the Wound of Amani'e'a, though a large part of the Ohi boarder leads on to the maelstrom sea, where it is fairly calm and noted for abundant fishing this far south. To the east and south the mysterious aurora of light from Mana'i'oa lands define their mutual boarders.

*Demographics*

The Ohi refuse to be counted, though their contributions range somewhere between 120 and 180 thousand warriors. They bring a strong contingent of healers and faith workers such as earth and air priests.

*Government*

Long before the great war the Ohi had a king over all their lands. Just prior to Totomuru's rule a series of visions warned the king and his tribal chiefs of an impending crusade. Once messages from the warlord arrived, the Ohi quickly signed on to his banner. The king rules by right of birth, though genealogy is difficult to ascertain in what was predominantly a non-writing culture for millennia.

## Mana'i'oa (Ma-NA-i-OH-ah)

TotoMuru, Jindalessa, Ki-Taieri, & Posk are from here.

### Overview

Again respected for their harsh and violent culture, the Mana'i'oa are nevertheless a surprisingly rich and vibrant people. It is interesting to note that Posk is from this nation.

### Nature

The southernmost tribe of the trolls is in the temperate zone of Mya. Their western lands are divided from the Ohi by strange natural phenomenon known as the Wall of Light (aka Wound of Amani'e'a), a shifting aurora of green, white and blue that few dare cross. The Wound divides them from their northwestern neighbours the Takaniki. Their nation presses up against the Bounteous Shallowsea to the north and east, and is pressed against a dry and sandy desert to the south and west. Cool all year around, especially in the north, some summer days can be very hot and humid.

Strange beasts roam the Mana'i'oa lands, giant man-eating birds, faceless creatures, and nameless monsters to cite a few. Portals to the monster realm are noted here.

### Demographics

With little argument, the Mana'i'oa vie with the Sahani'ea as the most violent, warlike and confronting of all troll peoples. It is said TotoMuru did not even subject some of the viler tribes, leaving them in isolation even

     By Dr Joe Ireland

unto this day. They present 220,000 capable troll warriors to the horde, though this is an overrepresentation of their numbers due to their eagerness to battle.

The Mana'i'oa bring to the horde a tribal war shout, popular among all the troll hordes, which has proven particularly effective against the moral of enemy forces.

*Government*

Prior to TotoMuru, all Mana'i'oa tribes answered only to their tribal chiefs. TotoMuru conquered the other tribes and installed himself as their first great chief of the council of chiefs, similar to an emperor. The council of chiefs has operated ever since, convening each troll council since then. There has been no great chief since TotoMuru, though Ki-Tieri would have claimed the title if he'd earned the right to wield the spear of the troll king.

 By Dr Joe Ireland

Choice, set free

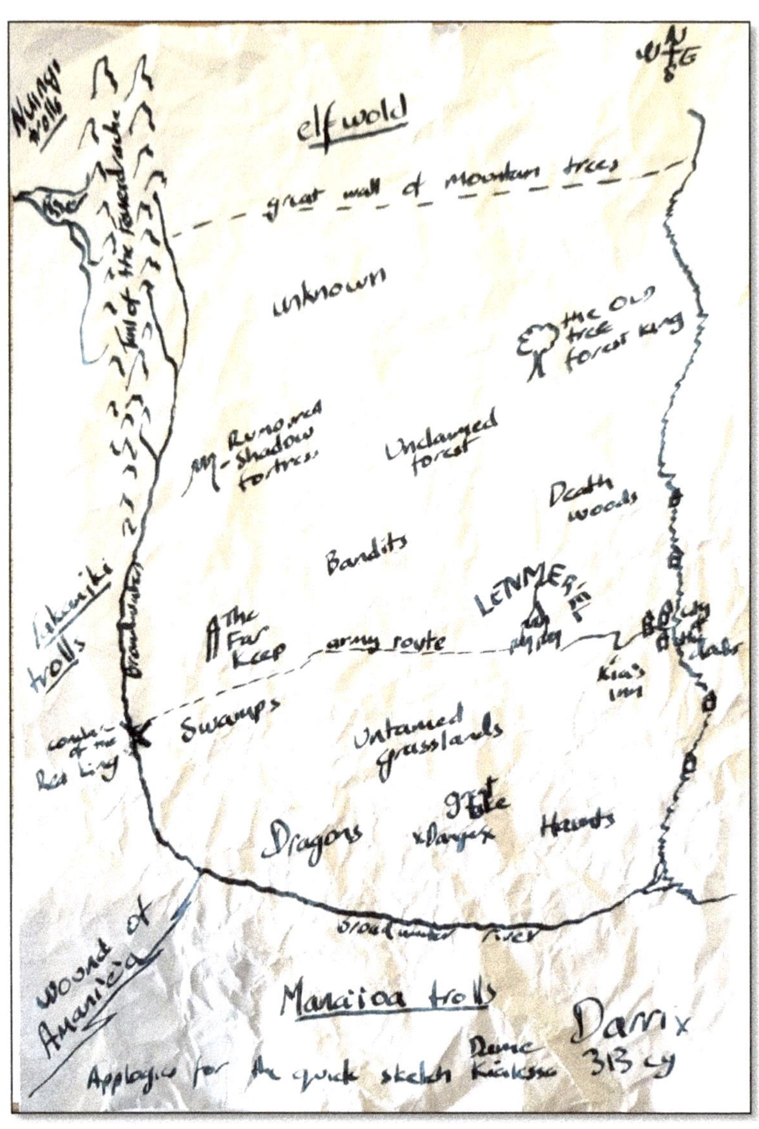


13 Darrix's map for Kialessa, drawn en route to the conclave of the Red King. 1/3 width ~4 journeys (see 'wizard's apprentice) except on roads where it equals 1 journey.

 By Dr Joe Ireland

Choice, set free

By Dr Joe Ireland

# Choice set free, book 6: Khozmoh Djinn & The Tae'anaryn

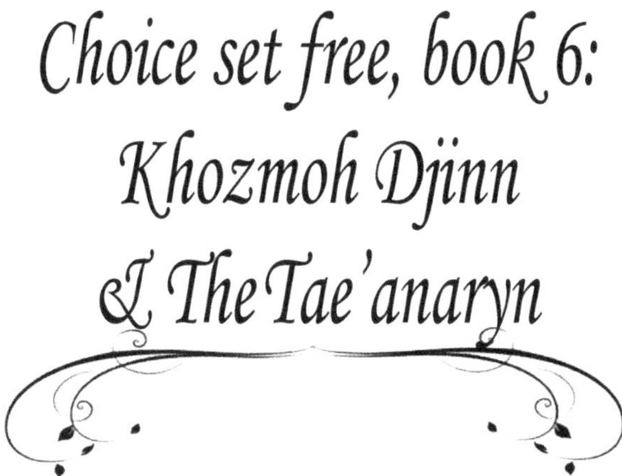

Life changes, but what if everything you ever believed turned out to be a lie? With every goodness taken away from her, how will Kialessa find herself in a cruel and distant world?

Or will she finally discover for herself why it was that her father would never speak of when he told the old stories of 'the lands beyond the mountains'…

Place the date and your personal mark here each
time you read this book – libraries included!

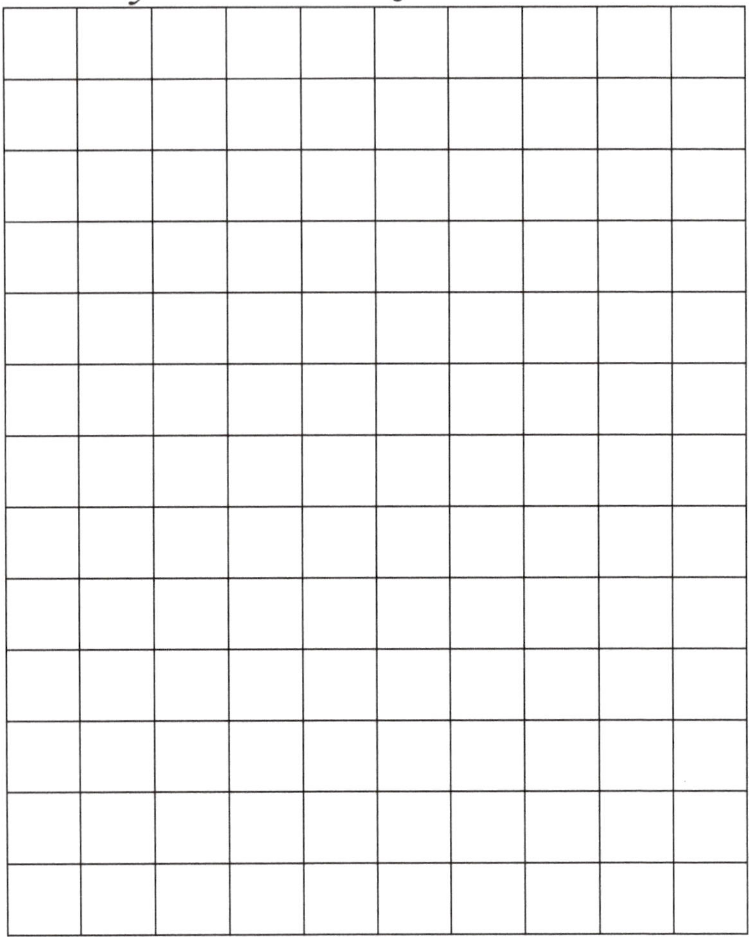

Why not share your experiences and thoughts with the
fandom! Get a grownup's permission and visit

## www.DrJoe.id.au

for fan art, sequels, competitions and more!

 By Dr Joe Ireland